"**Fushigi Yûgi** ("The Mysterious Play") is a sweeping saga; part fantasy, part historical romance and part action-adventure.... **Yû Watase** has an excellent grasp of characterization and writes great subtext to fill out her players.... Watase is a talented storyteller, as heavy scenes are leavened with love affairs, plot twists and swashbuckling battles."

Wizard Magazine

"Watase's storytelling is an engaging one. She paces her story well and knows when to pump up the energy. I even get a kick out of the 'letters to her readers' that she inserts into each chapter."

Tony Isabella, Comics Critic

"This is a charming, exciting romp through time and imagination... a well-told adolescent-female fantasy. Most U.S. comics, of course, are adolescent-male fantasics, so it offers a nice balance and should attract readers who've digested **Sailor Moon** and want to move on to something more mature."

Comics Buyer's Guide

ANIMERICA EXTRA GRAPHIC NOVEL

fushigi yûgi™

The Mysterious Play
VOL. 1: PRIESTESS

This volume contains the FUSHIGI YÛGI installments from Animerica Extra Vol. 1, No. 1 through Vol. 2, No. 4 in their entirety.

STORY & ART BY YÛ WATASE

English Adaptation/Yuji Oniki
Touch-Up Art & Lettering/Bill Spicer
Cover Design/Hidemi Sahara
Layout & Graphics/Carolina Ugalde
Editor/William Flanagan
Managing Editor/Annette Roman

V.P. of Editorial/Hyoe Narita
Publisher/Seiji Horibuchi
V.P. of Sales & Marketing/Rick Bauer

Printed in Canada

Published by Viz Communications, Inc.
P.O. Box 77010, San Francisco, CA 94107

10 9 8
First printing, August 1999
Fifth printing, June 2001
Sixth printing, November 2001
Seventh printing, May 2002
Eighth printing, October 2002

FUSHIGI YÛGI GRAPHIC NOVELS TO DATE

VOLUME 1 : PRIESTESS
VOLUME 2: ORACLE
VOLUME 3: DISCIPLE
VOLUME 4: BANDIT
VOLUME 5: RIVAL
VOLUME 6: SUMMONER

ANIMERICA EXTRA GRAPHIC NOVEL

fushigi yûgi™

The Mysterious Play

VOL. 1: PRIESTESS

Story & Art By

YÛ WATASE

CONTENTS

MODERN JAPAN AND A CHINA THAT NEVER WAS

The story of *Fushigi Yûgi* ("The Mysterious Play") takes place in two different worlds—present-day Japan and a version of ancient China that can be found in the romantic Chinese epics.

The main character of our story, Miaka, is a junior-high-school student who, like every other Japanese student her age, must pass a difficult test to enter the school of her choice. The better a reputation the school has, the harder the entrance exam. For that purpose, students in their third and final year of junior high become very serious about their studies and not only engulf themselves in their school work, but also go to evening "cram schools" where they take even more classes directed at passing their examinations.

The fantasy world of the book, *The Universe of the Four Gods*, is based on classics of Chinese literature such as *The Romance of the Three Kingdoms* and many other tales of adventure and magic written nearly two thousand years ago. It is an age where warring states vie for control of the most advanced civilization in the ancient world, and young emperors have inherited regimes that have been passed down from their forefathers in an unbroken line spanning thousands of years. It is a world of beauty and danger, and to enter, you have but to turn the page....

The Universe of the Four Gods is based on ancient China, but Japanese pronunciation of Chinese names differs slightly from their Chinese equivalents. Here is a short glossary of the Japanese pronunciation of the Chinese names in this graphic novel:

CHINESE	JAPANESE	PERSON OR PLACE	MEANING
Xong Gui-Siu	*Sô Kishuku*	*Tamahome's name*	*Demon Constellation*
Hong-Nan	*Konan*	*Southern Kingdom*	*Crimson South*
Gong Wu	*Kyûbu*	*A clue*	*Palace Strength*
Tai Yi-Jun	*Tai Itsukun*	*An oracle*	*Preeminent Person*
Kang-Lin	*Kôrin*	*A lady of Hong-Nan*	*Peaceful Jewel*
Daichi-San	*Daikyokuzan*	*A mountain*	*Greatest Mountain*

MIAKA

A chipper junior-high-school glutton who is trying to get into the exclusive Jonan High School to please her mother.

YUI

Miaka's best friend and a very intelligent girl who is certain to get into Jonan High School easily.

MIAKA'S MOM

A divorced single-mother who is trying to see that her children get the best education available.

KEISUKE

Miaka's kind, college-student brother.

HOTOHORI

A beautiful noble of ancient China who lives in the palace.

TAMAHOME

A dashing miser from ancient China.

KANG-LIN

An amazingly strong prospective bride for the emperor of the country of Hong-Nan in ancient China.

CHAPTER ONE
THE YOUNG LADY OF LEGENDS

ALL MY FAVORITES!!
WOW. I DON'T BELIEVE IT.
YUM
YUM
GIVE UP, MIAKA YŪKI. EATING IS A WASTE OF ENERGY FOR STUDENTS STUDYING FOR THEIR HIGH SCHOOL ENTRANCE EXAMS.
HA HA HA HA
URK
YOU MUST ONLY STUDY!!
WSK
WHAT THE--
WSK
HUH?

ANSWER, YŪKI !!
G--
NOW YOU MUST STUDY !
RECITE ALL THE MATH FORMULAS !
LIST EVERY SINGLE ENGLISH WORD STARTING WITH "A" !
TMP

GIMME BACK MY FOOD !!
YOU AWFUL GHOSTS! GIMME BACK MY PIZZA, MY NOODLES, MY CAKE, MY ETC. !!
WOMP
WOMP
MIAKA!
THAT WAS THE TEACHER !!
TPP
WHAT !?

DINNNGG DONNNGG

WELL, WHADDA YA KNOW...

...A DREAM!!

HEY YUI, I NEED TO COPY YOUR NOTES FROM PART OF TODAY'S CLASS THAT I SLEPT THROUGH.

MIAKA, AREN'T YOU GOING TO EAT ANYMORE?

NOPE! GOT CRAM SCHOOL TO ATTEND! I'M NOT HUNGRY ANYWAY! YOU FINISH IT OFF!

SEE YA

NOT HUNGRY? SHALL WE ASSESS THE DAMAGE HERE?
BUT WHY IS MIAKA GOING FOR...
SHE SAID SHE WANTED TO ATTEND YOTSUBADAI HIGH SCHOOL WITH US.
EEEEEP
CITY CENTRAL LIBRARY
BUS
CHASED BY DOZENS OF TEACHERS IN YOUR DREAM?
WHAT'S THAT MEAN?
SKRB SKRB
LATELY I'VE BEEN STAYING UP LATE STUDYING...
I KNOW YOU'RE DOING THIS FOR YOUR MOM, BUT YOU GOTTA TAKE IT EASY.

THERE'S NO WAY I'LL GET INTO JONAN.
WHEN SHE SAID, "I CAN'T WAIT TO SEE YOU IN THE JONAN HIGH SCHOOL UNI-FORM"...
...I COULDN'T TELL HER THAT I WANTED TO GO TO YOTSU-BADAI.
SWIF SWIF...
KREEEEK
DO NOT ENTER
RESTRICTED PRIVATE LIBRARY

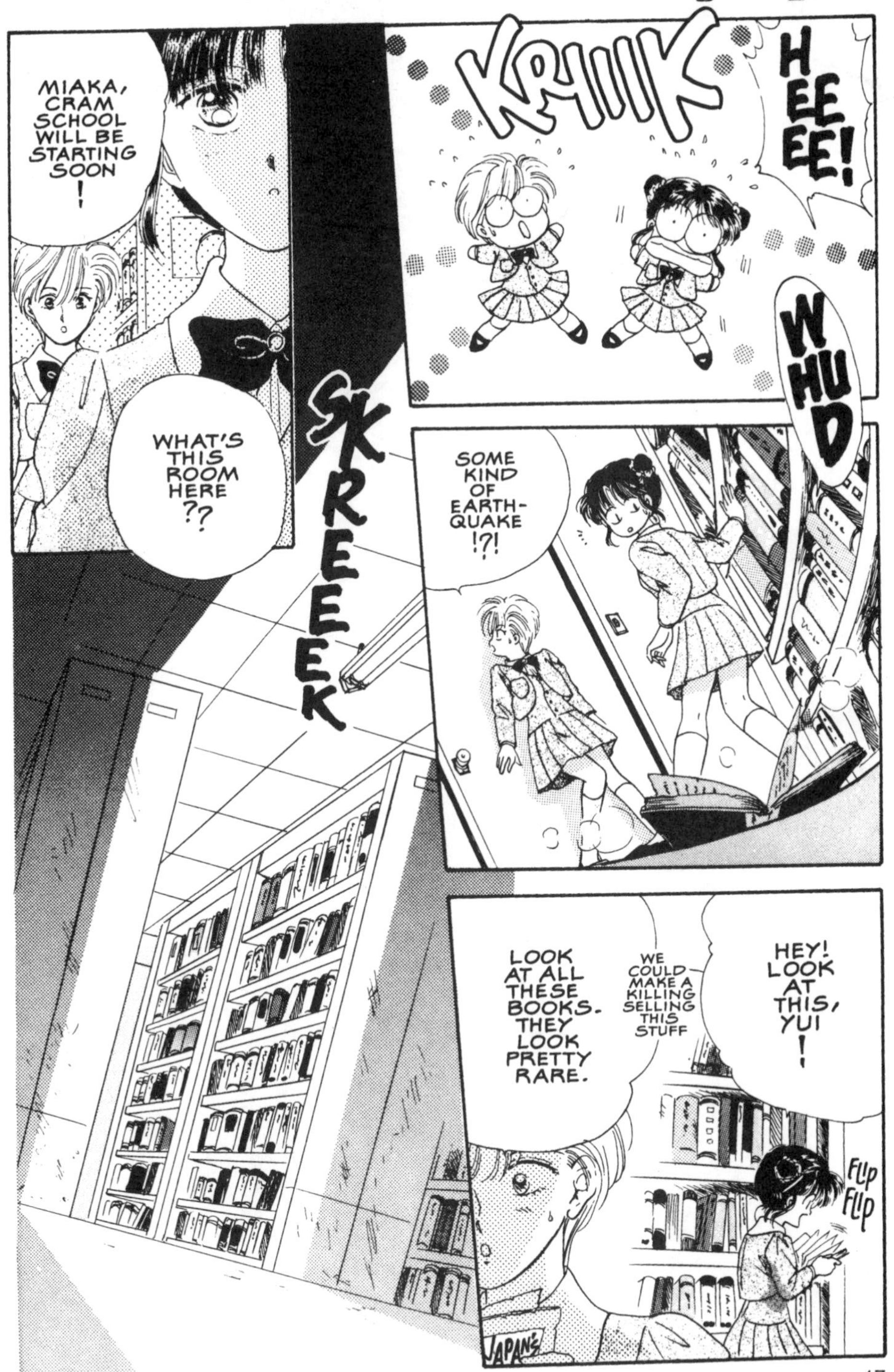
KRUNK
HEEEEEE!
MIAKA, CRAM SCHOOL WILL BE STARTING SOON!
WHAT'S THIS ROOM HERE??
SKREEEEK
WHUD
SOME KIND OF EARTH-QUAKE!?!
HEY! LOOK AT THIS, YUI!
WE COULD MAKE A KILLING SELLING THIS STUFF
LOOK AT ALL THESE BOOKS. THEY LOOK PRETTY RARE.
FLIP FLIP
JAPAN'S

THE UNIVERSE OF THE FOUR GODS. WHAT THE HECK?!
The Universe of the Four Gods
Japanese Translation by Einosuke Okuda
IT LOOKS LIKE A JAPANESE TRANSLATION OF SOME CHINESE LEGEND.
LEMME SEE.
Herein contains the tale of a young lady and her quest to gather the seven Constellations of Suzaku together.
And if you, the esteemed reader, should read to the story's end, the spell contained within this book shall bestow upon you the powers of the heroine, and grant you your wish.
WHAT'S A SUZAKU??
I DUNNO. A SORT OF PEACOCK, I GUESS...
The Universe of the Four Go
WHAT'S A SUZAKU??
I DUNNO. THIS HAS GOTTA BE SOME KIND OF SPELL BOOK.

WHAT'S A SUZA-KU--
WAK
I DON'T KNOW AL-READY!!
YOU DEAF ?!?
For indeed the moment the page is turned, the story will become reality.
SO-- SO IF YOU READ IT YOUR WISH COMES TRUE? SIGN ME UP!
YEAH RIGHT. AND I'M THE POPE IN ROME.
RRRR
ZHAAN
AIIII EEEE EE!!!
WHUD
WHUD WHUD

YUI... IT LOOKS LIKE IT'S OVER.
PHEW
GOOD! I JUST HATE EARTH-QUAKES.
WHUD...
!!!!
...FWEEEEEEE

EEEEE
MIAKA...
WHERE... ARE... WE... ??

OKAY, I CAN HANDLE THE LIBRARY BEING GONE. BUT THERE'S NO HÄAGEN DAZS, MISTER DONUTS, OR DENNY'S HERE!

IS FOOD ALL YOU EVER THINK ABOUT ?!?

WHHMPP...

SHE'S A JEWEL!
WE'LL MAKE A KILLING OFF HER!
HEH HEH HEH
YUI!?
AIIEE!!
WHO ARE THESE GUYS!?
WHY, YOU LITTLE TWIRP!!
WE'RE SLAVERS!!
WHAT!?!
MIAKA! YOU COULD HELP.
TWWIRRIRL
NICE OUTFIT! ARE YOU GUYS DANCERS?

HURRY!
MIAKA!
KOFF KOFF
KOFF
UMP
GO, YUI! RUN!!
EH...
YUI... RUN!
WHAP
LET GO OF ME! YOU LITTLE BRAT!!

STOP IT!
URRGH...
SCRATCH

SHADDUP AND GET--
KKRRRAK
ARRRGH!
MY ARM! YOU BROKE MY ARM!!
LET'S GET OUTTA HERE!!
POIT
WSK
ARE YOU ALL RIGHT? YOU'RE BLEED-ING.
WHAT'S WITH THIS GUY... HE'S GOT SOME-THING WRITTEN ON HIS FORE-HEAD.
SHFF SHFF
TH-THANK YOU SO MUCH!

SKIP THE THANKS. I'LL TAKE MONEY!
HUH?

URK
WE DON'T HAVE A CENT.
WE USED IT UP AT THE BURGER JOINT.
WHAT? YOU'RE BROKE !?!

TSK TSK TSK
DON'T YOU LADIES KNOW THAT MONEY MAKES THE WORLD GO AROUND ?!?
I'M NOT GIVING OUT ANY FREE RIDES !

NOBODY ASKED YOU TO SAVE US !
POOR FOLKS BUG ME! LATER !!

ZHANN ZHANN
W-WAIT! WHERE ARE WE...
MIAKA! IT'S ANOTHER EARTH-QUAKE !!

AIEEEEE!!
KAKKAKAK
BOOSHHAATT
HEY! WE'RE JUST BACK THE LIBRARY!
DID WE GET KNOCKED OUT??
PFEW
HUH?
JEEEN
OH GREAT! NOW I'M LATE FOR CRAM SCHOOL!

Hello. It's me Watase, and I'll be using this space to chat a little. I know I know. You're complaining about my bad handwriting, sorry but I just scribble stuff down. (Bad handwriting approximated for the English edition—Ed.) I don't like writing by hand. But since my writing is difficult enough to read I've decided to take some pains to write more legibly. yeah right.

Now let's see "Fushigi Yugi"... When I was eighteen, before I got published I looked up this incredibly thick "Buddhist Philosophy Encyclopedia" and was delighted to find how the character for "Oni" was read as "Tamahome." I discovered that "when the light of the Tamahome star in Suzaku's seven southern star constellations (out of a total of 28 constellations) fades, it is a sign of a bad harvest." As I came across this information I came up with the idea for this story. I thought up the characters of Tamahome 鬼宿 and Hotohori 星宿, but Miaka still wasn't part of the picture. (I wanted to use the character for star rather than constellation which would make Tamahome 鬼星 (pronounced Kisei) but that would have made Hotohori 星星 (pronounced Seisei) so I decided against it). I submitted the "FY" story idea along with my "Shishunki Miman Okotowari" (No Interest in Prepubescence) idea. "Shishunki" was accepted instead of "FY".

Although I've done my share of research on China for this story, it's still not a Chinese story. "FY" departs significantly from some basic historical facts. So please don't read it as if it were Chinese history. Who would? (For example, the emperor calls himself "Chin" so I decided against him using his real name.) I just want to let you know that I haven't been delinquent in my research. I read through 10 books before I began working on this serial. If there are any discrepancies they're being made with my knowledge.

ALL RIGHT! YOU HAVE TWO MONTHS TILL YOUR ENTRANCE EXAMS !!
THIS IS WHERE THE GOING GETS TOUGH. WILL YOU BE LAUGHING OR CRYING THIS SPRING? IT'S ALL DECIDED HERE!

THAT WAS TOO WEIRD TO BE A DREAM.
MAYBE IT WAS A HALLUCIN-ATION CAUSED BY EXAM ANXIETY.
DOUBTFUL.
WAA KKK
SO NOT ONLY ARE YOU LATE, BUT YOU'RE DAY-DREAMING TOO, EH, MIAKA?

YOU THINK YOU CAN GET INTO JONAN? YOU'LL HAVE TO BE IN THE TOP 75 PERCENTILE OR YOU WON'T STAND A CHANCE!
HARD LOVE
ONLY 30% OF THE APPLICANTS GET ACCEPTED! DO YOU STILL THINK THIS SPRING'S GOING TO BE A CAKEWALK?
HMM?

I'LL BET YOU DIDN'T HEAR A WORD I SAID!
FWAP
"LISTEN CAREFULLY! DAICHU PREP SCHOOL HAS *NEVER* TURNED OUT A STUDENT WHO FAILED THEIR EXAMS."
"NEVER RUIN YOUR MORALE BY WHINING ABOUT HOW YOU'RE GOING TO FAIL!"
"ALL RIGHT! YOU HAVE TWO MONTHS TILL YOUR ENTRANCE EXAMS!!"
"THIS IS WHERE THE GOING GETS TOUGH. WILL YOU BE LAUGHING OR CRYING THIS SPRING? IT'S ALL DECIDED HERE!"
"EVERYONE ELSE TAKING THE EXAM IS YOUR ENEMY! KILL OR BE KILLED! THIS IS WAR"--
THA-- THAT'S ENOUGH!!
ALWAYS THE SAME STUPID SPEECH!
HARD LOVE
HUMPH! AND THE NIGHT BEFORE THE TEST, YOU CAN ALWAYS PRAY!

IT'S NOT LIKE I'M TAKING THE JONAN EXAM 'CAUSE I WANT TO.
I WISH THERE WAS A GOD I COULD PRAY TO!
FAMILLE KISHIWA
GIMME ANOTHER.
Jeez! THAT'S YOUR THIRD BOWL. WHERE DO YOU PUT IT ALL?
!?
HEY, YOU'RE MAJORING IN CHINESE PHILOSOPHY, RIGHT? YOU EVER HEAR OF "THE UNIVERSE OF THE FOUR GODS"?
NOPE... I KNOW ABOUT THE FOUR GODS, THO.
WELL, TODAY AT THE LIBRARY...
YOUR TEST SCORES ARE IN FROM THE LAST TRIAL EXAM, MIAKA.
SPUTTZ
YOU'RE DOING BETTER BUT STILL NOT GOOD ENOUGH FOR JONAN.
NOW I WOULDN'T TELL YOU EVEN IF I KNEW...

YOU'LL BE JUST FINE, I KNOW YOU'LL DO IT FOR ME, RIGHT?
OF COURSE !!
HAHAHAHAHA

UMM... MOM, YOTSUBADAI IS REALLY WHERE...

PASS YOUR ENTRANCE EXAM !!
OOOPS!
GOTTA FINISH THIS DIARY ENTRY AND GET BACK TO STUDYING. "FOUND A STRANGE BOOK IN THE LIBRARY..." AND...
AND THEN...

YOU'VE GROWN INTO SUCH A FINE YOUNG WOMAN! AS A SINGLE PARENT, YOU'RE MAKING ME PROUD!

AAARRRGH! MY ARM!
STOP IT !!!
KRTCH
ARE YOU ALL RIGHT, MY LOVELY ?
THIS FLASHBACK HAS BEEN EDITED FOR CONTENT.
OH, YES!
THAT BOY IN MY DREAM... HE HAD THE CHINESE CHARACTER FOR DEMON WRITTEN ON HIS FOREHEAD.
HE WAS TALL AND KINDA GOOD LOOKING.
BUT A MONEY GRUBBER.
Then I met someone who was too greedy, but god was he gorgeous!!
WHOOPS! GOTTA STUDY TO KEEP MOM HAPPY !
BONG BONG
MIAKA, I'VE BROUGHT YOU A SNACK.
URK

MIAKA! LET'S HIT THE LIBRARY AGAIN...??
IT'S JUST THAT BOOK...THAT DREAM, TOO...I JUST CAN'T GET THEM OFF MY MIND!
SORRY, GOTTA PASS. THERE'S AN EXAM AT CRAM SCHOOL!
YUI'S GOT IT GOOD. SHE CAN GET BY WITHOUT STUDYING SO MUCH. I'D DIE TO GO, BUT...
VEEP
SIGH
THE STREETS ARE FILLED WITH COUPLES IN LOVE...
LOOK AT THOSE TWO, WALKING ARM-IN-ARM AT THEIR AGE!

HUH !?!
M-MOM !?
STOMP
TMP
WHAT ARE YOU DOING HERE? AREN'T YOU SUPPOSED TO BE AT WORK?!
KITAH DESIG
2F
DAICHU PREPARATORY SCHOOL
TMP
TMP
HER LOVER? IMPOSSIBLE !!
WHO IS THAT MAN ?!?
TMP
TM

SHE NEVER MENTIONED ANYTHING ABOUT ANOTHER MAN AFTER THE DIVORCE.

TAK TAK

Hello? Earth to Miaka!

I CAN'T BELIEVE THIS!

CHUD

I'M HOME.

MIAKA!

WHERE WERE YOU!? I'VE BEEN WORRIED SICK--!!

M-MOM?

YOU'RE SEEING A *MAN*, AREN'T YOU?

AH-- AH--
GHSP
I SUSPECTED SOMETHING WAS UP WITH YOU!
MOM! HOW COULD YOU!?
YOU READ MY DIARY...??
YOU SHOULD TALK! YOU'RE JUST A JUNIOR HIGH STUDENT AND HERE YOU ARE DATING SOME BOY! WITH YOUR EXAMS COMING UP TOO!
I'M NOT DATING! I JUST--

YOU PROBABLY DIDN'T GO TO CRAM SCHOOL TONIGHT! I'LL BET YOU WERE WITH HIM!
MOM, IF YOU'D JUST LISTEN--
NO, YOU LISTEN TO ME. YOU'LL NEVER GET INTO JONAN AT THIS RATE!
WHAT'LL THE NEIGHBORS SAY!? THINK OF MY REPUTATION--
I DON'T WANT TO GO TO JONAN!!
YOU'RE THE ONE WHO WANTS ME TO GO! I CAN'T PASS IT, SO YOU CAN JUST TAKE THE EXAM FOR ME!!
I'M TIRED OF PLAYING YOUR AGENDA!!

THWKK
WWKK
SO... WHAT IF I *DID* MEET SOME GUY...
...WHO ARE YOU TO CRITI-CIZE??

URGH. I'M STARVIN'...
I'M HOME.
YOU'RE SEEING A MAN YOURSELF, RIGHT!?
CHUD
AAARRRGH!
MIAKA!

KA-SHAM
ZOOP
MIAKA!
GIVE ME A BREAK!!
YOU COULDN'T CARE LESS HOW I FEEL!!
EVERY DAY, STUDY STUDY STUDY!
MIAKA, LET'S GO SEE A CONCERT.
SORRY, I GOT CRAM SCHOOL.
I WANT TO HAVE FUN! I WANT TO SLEEP! BUT I DON'T!
YOU CAN'T SIT DOWN UNTIL THE PROBLEM'S SOLVED.
NO MATTER WHAT I WANT, I KEEP ON STUDYING!

HOW'D I GET TO THE LIBRARY ??

I DID IT ALL JUST TO MAKE YOU HAPPY.

CITY CENTRAL LIBRARY

THE LIBRARIAN ISN'T HERE.

THE BOOK... IT'S STILL OPEN.

I'LL STAY HERE! A LITTLE WORRYING WILL DO MOM GOOD!

KA-THD

SO YOU READ THIS BOOK TO THE END, AND YOU GET A WISH, HMM?

WHEN PIGS FLY. BUT I MIGHT AS WELL JUST KILL SOME TIME READING IT.

I WISH MY PROBLEMS WOULD DISAPPEAR. PROBLEMS WITH THE ENTRANCE EXAMS... PROBLEMS WITH MOM...
I WISH I WERE PRETTY, SMART AND POPULAR WITH THE BOYS, LIKE YUI...

I WISH I HAD A GOOD-LOOKING BOY-FRIEND...
GAK!
WHY'D I JUST THINK OF *HIM?* HE WAS JUST A *DREAM*.
BLUSHH

W-W-WHY...
EHHH--??
Despite the shaking in her knees, the young lady lunges at the slavers. At that very moment, a gallant young man who bore the character for demon on his forehead saved the two young ladies...
BA-DUMP
BA-DUMP
a gallant young man who bore the character for demon on his forehead saved
BA-DUMP
WHY IS EVERYTHING IN MY DREAM WRITTEN RIGHT HERE--?
BA-DUMP

M-
MOM...
DING
DING
THE LIBRARY IS NOW CLOSING...
TMP
TMP
BE SURE TO GATHER ALL YOUR BELONGINGS BEFORE YOU LEAVE...
KRAK
The Universe of the Four Gods
Japanese Translation by Einosuke Okuda

FLIP FLIP
AND THUS THE YOUNG LADY OF LEGENDS OPENED THE DOOR TO ANOTHER WORLD, AND LIKEWISE BEGAN OUR TALE.

CHAPTER TWO

THE BOY WITH THE DEMON STAR

CITY CENTRAL LIBRARY
BLIIPP
RESTRICTED PRIVATE
young lady of
held the book in
trembling hands, she
gazed upon the words which
would transport her to the
other world. A world in
which she may be able to
fulfill her wish. The light
sparkled and flashed around
her, and lifted her gently,
but inexorably into the air.
It seemed to the young lady
as if the Earth itself had
from its foundations
engulfed her into undu-
lations of temporal and
indistinction.
young lady slipped
into a slumber, as
the welling con-
permeated her
it could be
it brought no
a steady
the calm-
found in the
parent, or
a horse-
its way
road.
HM?
CLAK
CLIK
CLAK
CLIK
WOOSH

WHA--
CLIK CLAK
CLAK
CLIK
WHAT AM--
CLAK

THAT'S RIGHT! I WAS AT THE LIBRARY, READING *THE UNIVERSE OF THE FOUR GODS*...
...AND I WAS SUCKED INTO THE BOOK!!

WHAT'LL I DO? WHAT'LL I DO? WHAT'LL I DO??
KAW
KAW
I'VE GOT TO GET BACK HOME!

OH...

THE LAST TIME I WAS HERE WITH YUI, WE MADE IT BACK, NO PROBLEM. NO WORRIES.
GO FER BROKE! I'LL JUST STAY HERE!
CAN'T GO HOME AFTER THAT FIGHT WITH MOM!
OKAY, MIAKA, WHAT ARE YOU GONNA DO WHEN YOU GET BACK?
CLAK
CLAK
CLIK
CLIK
NOW THAT I'VE DECIDED THAT...
CLAK-AK CLAK-AK
TUMP
THERE AIN'T NOBODY THAT HAND-SOME BACK HOME!
AND SINCE I'M HERE ANYWAY, I'LL FIND THAT BOY!

WOW!!
I'M IM-PRESSED!!
IT LOOKS LIKE A MOVIE SET!!
HUH??
HEY..
IT'S HIM!!
EX-CUSE ME..

WOW. LOOK AT THIS SETUP!
SOME KINDA CARNIVAL ??
EVERY-BODY'S SO BUSY! GOING EVERY WHICH-WAY!
SUCH STRANGE CLOTHES !!
WHO'S THAT !?!
STARE STARE
DIZZZ
OH, NO! WHERE'D HE GO!?
WHERE'D HE GO-- !?
POIT

URRR
OHHH YEAH... I SKIPPED DINNER.
DRRRRL
YOU MIND!? I GOTTA KEEP THE PLACE CLEAN!
HEY, MISTER! I'M LOOKING FOR A GOOD-LOOKIN' GUY! HE'S GOT THE CHARACTER FOR DEMON WRITTEN ON HIS FOREHEAD.
A LITTLE OLDER THAN ME.
YOU LOOK MORE LIKE THE OWNER OF A GROCERY STORE NEAR ME.
CHOMP CHOMP
KLINK
WELL, YOU GOT A GOOD-LOOKIN' GUY RIGHT IN FRONT OF YOU!
HEY! WHAT THE HELL IS THIS MONEY !?!
AIIIEEE!
A JAPAN-ESE 100 YEN PIECE !!

TMP TMP
THERE'S NO SCHOOL... NO BLOWHARD TEACHER FROM SCHOOL...
TMP TMP
ULP ULP
TMP TMP
TMP TMP
SO... NO ONE KNOWS ME HERE.
TMP TMP
MNCH MNCH
TMP TMP
WA-HOO!
NO DEPRESSING CRAM SCHOOL, NO REPORT CARD ANXIETY, NO GLOOMY EXAMS!
I DON'T HAVE TO WORRY ABOUT MY MOTHER...
I'M FREE!!
Z-ING

FSSSAAGGH FSSSAAGGH

EXCUSE ME. I'M LOOKING FOR A BOY WITH DEMON ON HIS FOREHEAD.

HUH WHA--!? LOOKING FOR KOI WITH LEMON ON A BOAR'S HEAD?

CAN'T UNNERSTAND A WORD YER SAYIN'!

I CAN'T FIND HIM...

I WISH YUI OR MY BROTHER WERE HERE.

IT'S NOT AS MUCH FUN ALONE...

I'M GETTING KINDA TIRED. MAYBE I'LL GO HOME...

TUMP

GRIN...

I HAPPENED TO NOTICE YOU'RE ALONE. ME TOO. WANNA GO TO THE CARNIVAL WITH ME?
UM...
DOES THIS MEAN I'M...
...BEING PICKED UP !?!
YAAY! MY FIRST TIME!

MY FIFTEEN-YEAR BOYFRIEND-LESS EXISTENCE FINALLY COMES TO AN END!
SO NOW I'M WOMAN ENOUGH TO ATTRACT A MAN!
UM...
'SCUSE ME?

I'M SORRY BUT I'M BUSY LOOKING FOR SOMEONE, YOU SEE...
YADDA YADDA YADDA
OH, HE'S A FRIEND OF MINE!

I'LL TAKE YOU TO HIM.
HA HA HAAA!
'NOTHER BEER!
OVER HERE!

I JUST OVER-HEARD SOME-THING ABOUT...
...A GIRL WEARING FUNNY CLOTHES NEARBY!

WOOOSH
IS THAT TRUE ??
MNCH MNCH
WOAH!

I HEARD THIS RUMOR THAT SHE WAS LOOKING FOR SOME BOY WITH A DEMON ON HIS FOREHEAD.
POK
I NEVER HEARD OF 'IM.

AS LONG AS YOU PAY, I'LL DO JUST ABOUT ANYTHING.

IS SHE A GIRL IN A SHORT SKIRT WITH HER HAIR DONE IN BUNS, OR DID SHE HAVE SHORT HAIR?
HOW WOULD I KNOW? WHO'RE YOU ANYWAY ??

Oh! I'M SORRY. IF YOU'LL TAKE ONE OF THESE.
MY CARD.
JACK-OF-ALL-TRADES ?

So I just want to clarify some things about my background. It seems I have to inform EVERY reader that I'm a woman. ☺ As for how old I am... Because I'm pretty young I'm not embarrassed about my age. Suffice to say I first got published at 18 and then "Prepubescence" came out when I was 20. You do the math.

I've had fans who tell me, "I want to be a manga artist just like you." Don't be JUST like me! "Lately I've been copying your drawings so much they look like yours." Well I suppose that's all right as long as you eventually acquire your own style. Every artist is always influenced by somebody else in the beginning. But I don't think it's such a good idea to continue copying other artists after you get published. Although they may seem the same, there's a big difference between being a big fan of an artist and unconsciously resembling that style, or parody, or reference, AND PLAGIARISM. Lifting one or two ideas or scenes I can handle, but if you make a comic exactly like mine, I'll get mad at you!

I dunno, uh...

Now THAT'S something that can get me mad! (I'm still new to this.) I know that there are tons of ideas that resemble each other, but to steal an episode verbatim... And when I get upset it means I'm 10 times angrier than the average person. (Usually I'm laid back no matter what people say to me. Friends will say, "Why don't you get mad once in a while," and get mad at me!) Guess I haven't grown up. For the past two years, I haven't read any of my favorite manga artists who have influenced me! (Actually I haven't been reading much manga in general.) I want to shed my influences. I just want to draw manga my own way. But my drawings aren't getting better! And I'm working on it so hard!

SO YOU LIED TO ME.

WHAK

STOP IT!!!

HEY, THIS IS NO BETTER THAN HOME!

SKRCH SKRCH

IT'S YOUR FAULT FOR BEING SO NAÏVE!

THERE'RE DELIN-QUENTS IN THE BOOK, TOO--

AND IT WON'T END UP ON MY REPORT CARD.
WHOOOSH
WHAT THE HECK. THIS IS JUST A STORY.
I CAN DO ANYTHING I WANT TO!!
I THINK.
ALL RIGHT, TOUGH GUYS! DO YOU SEE THESE BCG VACCINATION TRACKS!?
NOW YOU'RE GONNA PAY!!
HUH?
I SAW THIS WOMAN'S PRO WRESTLING MOVE THREE DAYS AGO ON TV !!
GOOOGH
GAKK

WHAT'S HER DEAL ?!?
WAAHHH
THERE AIN'T NO MARTIAL ARTS SCHOOL THAT TEACHES *THAT* MOVE!!
WAK-KAM M
THUKK
THuKK
NOTE: THESE MOVES AREN'T SANCTIONED IN INTERNATIONAL COMPETITION.
PANT
BRING ON JESSE "THE BODY" VENTURA! I'M READY!
PANT
MY FIRST FIGHT.
DOES THIS GIRL GOT IT, OR WHAT !?!
PANT PANT PANT
WOFF
OWCHIE!

GRRB
YOU LITTLE-- NOW YOU'LL GET WHAT YOU DESERVE!!
WHUD HD
YAAAH!
THOPP
HELP ME..
ZHHTT
NO!
SHUT UP AND DO WHAT YOU'RE TOLD!!
GA-FORK
GA-FORK
NO!!
MOM! KEISUKE!!

ZHUMMP...
...!?
FIPP FIPP

I KNEW IT'D BE YOU! YOU'RE NOT WITH YOUR FRIEND THIS TIME?
SHUMP
CAN YOU...
...STAND ??
I WAS SCARED !!
SO SCARED!
JJIKK

SHHHT
SO YOU WERE LOOKING FOR ME?
HUH?
THAT'S RIGHT. I WANTED TO SEE YOU...
WHAT FOR?

DON'T SWEAT IT. I'VE GOT WORK TO DO, SO DON'T COME FOLLOWING ME.

GO ON HOME!

I CAN'T GO HOME AFTER THAT BIG FIGHT WITH MY MOM.

I COULDN'T EVEN IF I WANTED TO.

I DON'T WANT TO BE ALONE.

LOOK, YOU CAN'T KEEP HANGING ALL OVER ME LIKE THIS!
BUT IF I HELP YOU IN YOUR WORK, IT'S OKAY, RIGHT ?!?

SKRICH SKRACH
......
PLEASE PLEASE PLEASE

IF YOU'RE THAT DETER-MINED...
YOU SEE THAT FANCY PROCES-SION OVER THERE! THAT'S FOR THE EM-PEROR.
THE ONE IN THE CENTER IN THE GAUDIEST CARRIAGE IS THE EMPEROR OF HONG-NAN.

IF YOU COULD FETCH A COUPLE OF GEMS FROM THE EMPEROR'S CROWN, I'D BE ROLLING IN MONEY.
BUT SINCE THAT'S IMPOS-SIBLE, I'LL JUST BE MOSEY-ING ALONG...

VWAM
I'LL BE BACK WITH THE GEMS!
YOU THINK I WAS SERIOUS !?!
BWOINGG
IF I GET THEM, YOU'LL TAKE ME WITH YOU, RIGHT ??
!?
TMP TMP

SOMEBODY SAVED MY LIFE AND I GOTTA PAY HIM BACK! YOU CAN SPARE THEM! WHAT'S THE PROBLEM? HOLD ON A SEC!

...

UMM...

HEY!

NO ONE IS RUDE TO THE EM-PEROR !!

QUIT BEING SO PRISSY! IT AIN'T LIKE YOU'RE SOME DEBU-TANTE!

KILL HER !!

AARGH!
VSSH VSSH
WHHMRH
POFF POFF
RRMBL
YOU SOME KIND OF MORON!?
I DON'T BELIEVE IT!
FUDUD
KOFF KOFF
WINNIH WINNIH
ARE YOU TRYIN' TO GET KILLED ?!?
RRMBL
OH!
YOU SAVED ME AGAIN !?

I'M XONG GUI-SIU, BUT CALL ME BY MY NICKNAME, TAMAHOME. WHO'RE YOU?
UHHH... MIAKA YŪKI.
ALL RIGHT, MIAKA. YOU GOT GUTS, SO I'LL TAKE YOU UNDER MY WING FOR A WHILE.
THANKS... BUT THAT MEANS I HAVE TO GIVE YOU *THREE* GEMS NOW.
REALLY!? BUT YOU'VE SAVED ME *THREE* TIMES! I GOTTA GIVE YOU *SOME* REWARD.
YEAH... I'LL CLAIM MY REWARD NOW.

THERE THEY ARE!!
GO HOFF
KAFF
BAS-TARD! YOU'LL PAY FOR THAT!!
!?
KAFF
POP POP
BLUSH

ZHHAAAANNN
ZHHANANAN
HEY!!
FWOOOSH
JUST LIKE WHEN I CAME HERE...
...MY BODY'S DIS-APPEARING!!
FWOOOSH

I'M GOING BACK HOME!!
SHE'S VANISH-ING!!
ZHHAAANNN
YAAAHHHH!
ZHHAAAAANNN
SHE'S A MON-STER!!
YOUR MAJESTY! THAT GIRL IS DIS-APPEARING INTO THE RED LIGHT!!
BEEP BEEP BEEP BEEP
CITY CENTRAL LIBRARY

WOOSH
I JUST GOT TO KNOW HIM. I SHOULD AT LEAST GET A CHANCE TO SAY GOODBYE!
HOLD ON... THIS IS ALL TOO SUDDEN.
WOOSH
I SAID STOP IT!!
I GUESS I'M BACK.
OOOO OOOPS...
UH...

WHAT AM I!? AN ORDINARY JUNIOR HIGH STUDENT.
DETAIN THE GIRL AND THE YOUNG MAN.
HUH ?!
YES, SIRE !!
WHAT...
...ARE YOU ??
JAAAAAATTZZZ
TAMA-HOME... !!

CHAPTER
THREE
THE PRIESTESS
OF SUZAKU

Under the Emperor's orders, Tamahome and the Young Lady were imprisoned in the basement dungeon of the palace.
HEY KEISUKE, WHERE'S DADDY?
MIAKA, MOM AND DAD ARE DIVORCED.
DIVORST?
MOM...
DON'T BE SAD...

I'D DO ANYTHING TO MAKE YOU HAPPY, MOMMY.
SQUEZZ
SO DON'T LOOK SO SAD...
BUT I *AM* SO SAD!

"I'M FROM ANOTHER WORLD, AND I WAS SUCKED INTO SOME BOOK I FOUND IN THE LIBRARY."
YEAH, LIKE HE'LL BUY THAT.
WHAT'LL I TELL HIM? "WE'RE IN A BOOK."
WHERE'RE YOU FROM, ANY-WAY?
WHAT WAS THAT LIGHT COMING OUT OF YOUR BODY!?
SKTCH SKTCH
...
BUT IT LOOKS LIKE I CAN GO BACK AND FORTH BETWEEN WORLDS AS LONG AS THE BOOK'S OPEN.
...
SO WHAT'S UP WITH YOUR MOM? YOU WERE TOSSING IN YOUR SLEEP!
WELL, WHAT-EVER.

I HAVE NO IDEA WHAT THIS IS ABOUT...
I PROMISED MOM I'D DO ANYTHING TO MAKE HER HAPPY... AND THEN I SAID ALL THOSE AWFUL THINGS TO HER.
...BUT YOU SHOULDN'T BE TOO STUBBORN.
ZHANN
Y-Y-YOU'RE RIGHT... I GOTTA GO HOME AND APOLOGIZE.
SEE, ALL KIDS CARE ABOUT THEIR PARENTS.
AND ALL PARENTS CARE ABOUT THEIR KIDS.
THAT WAS A REALLY NICE THING TO SAY!
I'M IMPRESSED!
THAT'LL BE A FIVE MON COUNSEL-ING FEE!
SMAK

WHY HAVE YOU NOT PUT THEM TO DEATH YET !?!
ESPECIALLY THAT BIZARRE WOMAN! SHE EMITTED THAT STRANGE LIGHT AND ATTEMPTED TO VANISH!
SHE MIGHT BE AN EVIL SPIRIT, YOUR MAJESTY! NOW WITH YOUR PER-MISSION...
WE HAVE CAUSE TO WONDER...
...IF THAT GIRL MIGHT BE THE YOUNG LADY OF LEGENDS.
ONE MOMENT.

PROBLEM NUMBER ONE: HOW DO WE GET OUT OF HERE?
IMPOS-SIBLE !!
GLARE
I CAN GO HOME ANY TIME I'M IN A TIGHT SPOT, BUT I HAVE TO HELP TAMAHOME GET OUT OF HERE.
HEY! WHAT'D YOU JUST STICK IN YOUR MOUTH!? OUT WITH IT!
GLAARRE...
ALL RIGHT! SNACKS !!
CHOMM CHOMM
DO I HAVE ANY-THING THAT COULD HELP?
SHHT
WHAT, THIS ??
CHOMM CHOMM

WOAHH!
What the hell is that!?!
ZHOOP
?
GAK! G--G-GET IT AWAY FROM ME!!
FFANK KYUU!
HE PASSED OUT! WAY TO GO!!
GULMP
DWAM

A-- A--ARE YOU SURE I CAN HAVE IT!? THIS IS TOO GOOD TO BE TRUE!!
IT'S JUST GUM. GIVE IT A TRY.
BA-DUMP
BA-DUMP
BA-DUMP
BA-DUMP
NO WAY! I COULDN'T JUST EAT SOMETHING THIS PRECIOUS!!
I COULD GET ONE RYO FOR THIS! YOU HEAR? ONE RYO!!
KLUTCH
WHAT'S THE BIG DEAL?
TAMA-HOME! WHAT'S THIS BIRD?

THAT'S SUZAKU.
EVERYBODY KNOWS THAT.
SO THEY GOT A SHRINE HERE?
SUZAKU ??
OHHH YEAH. I REMEMBER SOMETHING ABOUT IT IN THE BOOK'S PROLOGUE.
IT'S ONE OF THE FOUR GODS... "SEIRYU," "BYAKKO," "SUZAKU," AND "GENBU."
SUZAKU IS OUR GOD. EACH OF THE THREE OTHER EMPIRES HAVE THEIR OWN GOD TO WORSHIP.
HM M?
POIT
WHAT A WONDERFUL SMELL...
SOMETHING'S COOKIN'!
WAFFL
WAFFL
GODS BLAH BLAH... EMPERORS BLAH BLAH...
...AT'S NOT IMPORTANT. WE GOT TO GET OUT OF HERE BEFORE WE'RE CAUGHT--
VWOOP

FWO-OHH

...

SNF SNF

TMP TMP

SNF SNF

ZHOOP

HUH ?
WHA-- ?
NOT A SCRAP
THAT FILLED ME UP.
NOW IT'S TIME TO GO BACK TO MY OWN WORLD.
URK!

Getting back to where we left off, I'm sure some of my work reminds the readers of other comics. Of course I never do it consciously! (Even I have some pride). Someone ends up pointing it out, and then I'm like "oh my god!" Wait. "Magical Nan" was different. That came from a book my editor gave me. Although I tried to make my version totally different, due to limitations on the number of pages, I was told to imitate the book. I really DO try not to copy scenes. During junior high and high school I was influenced mostly by people like Toyoo Ashida (Director, Animation Director: Yamato, Minky Momo and Vampire Hunter D) and Akemi Takada (Character Designer: Creamy Mami, Urusei Yatsura, Kimagure Orange Road) (my older drawings from "Prepubescence Vol. 3" I was really into Takada at the time) and Mutsumi Inomata (Character Designer: Windaria, Leda, Brain-Powerd), anime artists rather than comic artists. Now I hardly get a chance to watch animation at all, so I don't know what's going on these days. I really loved animation. Seems so long ago. I tried to cram these animation influences into a Shojo manga drawing style that never really existed before. (I've asked many people, and there's nobody else who draws like I do). I think that my own pictures are too complicated! It's really hard to find a balance. I have many fellow artists who can give me advice, but I just can't change at this point.

I was really into boys' comics so everyone thought I'd be writing for Shonen manga magazines such as Shonen Sunday. But do you think that maybe after three years of hard work, I finally managed to draw shojo manga effectively? ♥ *I still have a long way to go.* Okay, okay, I'm getting a little long winded here but most of my fan letters come from people who want to become comic artists, so you guys can use this as reference (maybe). To sum up, I recommend you study and incorporate all the elements of artists you admire in your unique way into your own drawings (without ripping them off). I tend to discard those elements that don't fit with my style. You should also read as many novels, see as many films and dramas as possible. Remember the great Osamu Tezuka once said, "If you want to write a new manga then don't bother reading another manga!" Of course, this is coming from someone who bought his "How to Draw Manga" AFTER getting published! *Sorry!*

My friends razzed me about it. But I don't know how to do effects work. So sue me!!

TEE HEE HEE
THE DOOR'S OVER THERE.
ALL THE BUILDINGS LOOK THE SAME AROUND HERE!
W-WHICH DOOR DID I COME THROUGH!? I'VE GOT TO FIND MY WAY BACK!
I CAN'T GO BACK HOME BEFORE HELPING TAMA-HOME ESCAPE!!
BU-WAANGG
I'M LOST! WHERE'S TAMA-HOME!?

WOW, SHE'S BEAUTIFUL!!
H-H-HELLO...
GAKK
SO YOU'RE THE GIRL THEY CAPTURED YESTERDAY?
YOU MUST BE MISTAKING ME FOR SOMEONE ELSE. I'M JUST AN ANONYMOUS PASSERBY.
NOW IF YOU'LL EXCUSE ME.
TMP TMP TMP
DON'T WORRY! DON'T WORRY!
SHHT
I'VE GOT NOTHING TO DO RIGHT NOW, SO HOW ABOUT I GIVE YOU THE GRAND TOUR OF THE PALACE?
THE SPECIAL NO-GUARD TOUR.
THE GUARDS WON'T HEAR ABOUT YOU FROM ME!

WHERE'D THAT IDIOT GO-- !?!
UH-OH...
GET THE GUARDS... I FOUND HIM!!
DAMN
THIS IS THE ONLY WAY!
MIAKA... I'LL LURE THEM AWAY WHILE YOU ESCAPE!
YOU NEED TO FIND YOUR COMPANION??

YOU CAME FROM... ANOTHER WORLD !?
I CAN'T GO BACK TO MY OWN WORLD UNTIL I KNOW HE GOT AWAY SAFELY...
HE WOULDN'T HAVE GOTTEN MIXED UP IN THIS IF IT WEREN'T FOR ME!
Y-YOU PROBABLY DON'T BELIEVE ME, AND I UNDER-STAND.
NOT AT ALL!
I JUST LOVE THINGS LIKE THAT!
HUH ?
WHY IS THIS HAPPENING ANYWAY!? I THOUGHT READING THIS BOOK WAS SUPPOSED TO LET ME ESCAPE FROM LIFE, EXAMS AND ALL THAT ROTTEN STUFF!
YOU MUST THINK I'M CRAZY.
UH-OH. I'LL BET SHE THINKS I'M A LOONY AND IS LEADING ME STRAIGHT TO THE GUARDS.

TOUCHIE FEELIE
TOUCHIE FEELIE
TOUCHIE FEELIE
TOUCHIE FEELIE
THAT'S INCREDIBLE!
AM I SOME KINDA SIDE-SHOW FREAK?!?
STOP TALKING ABOUT GOING AWAY, AND STAY HERE A WHILE.
TWNKL
I JUST KNOW THE EMPEROR WOULD NEVER HAVE YOU KILLED.
OH...I'M MIAKA YŪKI. JUST CALL ME MIAKA.
I'M "HOTOHORI," ALTHOUGH PEOPLE USUALLY CALL ME SOME-THING ELSE.
BA-DUMP...
J-JEEZ, MY HEART'S POUNDING OVER A WOMAN...
WHAT'S THE MATTER?
EVERY-ONE SAYS THAT.
O-OH... I WAS JUST THINKING HOW BEAUTI-FUL YOU ARE!!
HA HA HA HA HA HA

SPILL IT! WHERE'S THE GIRL!?

BEATS ME.

AWWWWW

SHE GOT AWAY WHILE YOU GUYS WERE BUSY CHASING AFTER ME.

TOO BAD, HUH?

THOK

SO YOU WERE JUST SOME DECOY...!?

OWW!

FA-JASHHH

TAMA-HOME!!

OH NO!

GATCH
YOU IDIOT! WHY DIDN'T YOU GO HOME !?!
I CAN'T JUST LEAVE YOU !!
WHAT GOOD IS IT FOR YOU TO BE A DECOY!?
GUYS, COME AND CAPTURE ME INSTEAD!
THA-KAMMMMMMMM
Y-- YOU BAS-TARD !!
KONCH
OWCH

SHFF
LAY ONE FINGER ON THAT GIRL AND YOU'RE DEAD.
!
YOU LITTLE--
SILENCE!
YOU ARE NOT PERMITTED TO TOUCH THOSE TWO WITHOUT OUR DIRECT ORDER!
HOTO-HORI?

Y-Y-YOUR MAJESTY !!
JA-THUNK
HUH?
URK
IT'S FLAT !!
C'MON! HOW COULD A GIRL WHO'S SO YOUNG AND BEAUTIFUL BE THE EMPEROR?
GIVE ME A BREAK.
"GIRL"!? HIS MAJESTY IS ALL MAN !!
NOTHING ABOVE. A-AND BELOW IS SOME MYSTERIOUS OBJECT I KNOW NOTHING OF--
OH M'GOD
OH M'GOD
OH M'GOD
TOUCHIE
STOP THINKING ABOUT THAT RIGHT NOW !!

OUR APOLOGIES. TRICKERY WAS NOT OUR INTENTION.
WE SIMPLY WISHED TO UNDERSTAND YOU BETTER.
HE SEEMS LIKE A COMPLETELY DIFFERENT PERSON.
SITTING LIKE THIS IS KILLING ME...
OKAY...
AT LEAST WE'VE DISPROVED OUR COUNSELOR'S ASSERTION THAT YOU ARE EVIL SPIRITS.
AHEM!
SO THEN... YOU'RE GONNA LET US GO?
OF COURSE, YOU SHALL NOT BE EXECUTED.

PHEW! NOW I CAN GO HOME WITHOUT ANY REGRETS...
HOW-EVER... WE HAVE ONE REQUEST.
WILL YOU PROTECT OUR EMPIRE, *PRIESTESS OF SUZAKU*?
HUH?
WHERE WHERE ??
WE ARE REFERRING TO *YOU*, MIAKA.
THERE'S A LEGEND IN OUR LAND.
AT A TIME WHEN THE EMPIRE FALLS INTO DIS-ORDER AND IS ON THE VERGE OF COL-LAPSE...
...A YOUNG LADY WOULD APPEAR FROM ANOTHER WORLD SEEKING THE POWER OF SUZAKU.
THE MOMENT SHE POSSESSES THE POWER OF SUZAKU, SHE WILL LEAD THE EMPIRE TO GLORY.

THIS YOUNG LADY, CALLED THE PRIESTESS OF SUZAKU, HAS FINALLY ARRIVED. SHE SITS BEFORE US NOW.
Y-YOU--
YOU CAME SEEKING THE POWERS OF THE SUZAKU SO THAT YOUR WISH WOULD BE GRANTED, YES?
YET, YOU ARE A WOMAN WITH A WISH, CORRECT?
YOU'VE GOT IT ALL WRONG!!
I'M JUST A JUNIOR HIGH SCHOOL GIRL CRAMMING FOR MY EXAMS! I HAPPENED TO LAND IN YOUR WORLD BY MISTAKE!
Herein contains the tale of a young lady and her quest to gather the seven Constellations of Suzaku together.
BA-DUMP
BA-DUMP
BA-DUMP
THAT WAS...
And if you, the esteemed reader, should read to the story's end, the spell contained within this book shall bestow upon you the powers of the heroine, and grant you your wish.
BA-DUMP

I COULD BECOME A HOT BABE WHO LOOKS GOOD IN A TIGHT MINI-SKIRT!
OR HAVE ALL THE SCHOOL BOYS DESPERATELY IN LOVE WITH ME!
TO MY BELOVED MIAKA
LOVE
OR I COULD BE TOUGH ENOUGH TO BEAT UP ALL THE BULLIES AT SCHOOL!
OR EVERY MEAL COULD BE A FEAST, THREE TIMES A DAY!
MISTER, I AM INTO THIS!!
WHAT IS THIS GIRL BLABBERING ABOUT?
DOES THE READER OF THE UNIVERSE OF THE FOUR GODS BECOME THE HERO OF THE STORY?
The Universe of the Four Gods Japanese Translation by Einosuke Okuda
SO THEN THE GOD SUZAKU HAS THE POWER TO GRANT ANY WISH?
MIAKA'S IN SHOCK!!
B-BUT... ...MOST OF ALL...
...I COULD GET INTO WHATEVER SCHOOL I WANT TO...

chuckle
YOU'RE MUCH TOO MODEST.
HAVE YOU CON-SIDERED RULING THE WORLD?

EVERY-ONE, STAND BACK !!

THIS YOUNG LADY WILL OBTAIN THE POWER OF SUZAKU.

THE PRIESTESS OF SUZAKU, THE ONE WHO WILL PROTECT OUR EMPIRE, STANDS BEFORE YOU!

MRR MRR

HOPE I DON'T DIS-APPOINT.

YOU'RE MAKIN' TOO MUCH OF THIS!

I'M THERE! I'LL DO IT! I'LL BE YOUR PRIESTESS OF SUZAKU !!

MY LIFE HAS BEEN LEADING UP TO THIS !!

I-IS THAT SO?

WATCH IT!

THANK YOU...
YOUR EMINENCE, PRIESTESS OF SUZAKU.
...
SHU
UUSS HHH

PLEASE LOOK AFTER TAMA-HOME FOR ME!
OKAY. AND NOW I'LL BE HEADING ON HOME!
SEE YA!
THEY'RE TREATING ME LIKE I'M ALL HIGH AND MIGHTY!
EVEN TAMA-HOME'S BOWING!
WELL... AT LEAST MY WORRIES OVER MY ENTRANCE EXAMS ARE OVER!
WELL, YEAH... BUT FIRST I GOTTA APOLOGIZE TO MY MOM.
WHAT ARE YOU TALKING ABOUT? YOU JUST SAID...
AND I HAVE SCHOOL.
HEY! WHAT'S THIS BOOK DOING ON THE FLOOR?

LOOKS LIKE THE LOCK ON THIS DOOR IS BROKEN.
HUH ??
CITY CENTRAL LIBRARY
KA-CHAK KA-CHAK
SHFFL
WHAT'S THIS BOOK DOING HERE?
CITY CENTRAL LIBRARY
I'M HEARING VOICES IN MY HEAD...
"BOOK" !?!
IT'S THE LIBRARIAN! OH, NO! DON'T CLOSE THAT BOOK!!
IT'S COMING FROM OUTSIDE OF THE BOOK.
FLP FLP
?

LET'S HIT THE ROAD.
Y'KNOW, IT'S COLD IN HERE.
I'LL HAVE THE LOCK FIXED TOMORROW. DON'T WANT ANYBODY GETTING IN HERE.
WHUD
The
niverse
of the
our Gods
Japan
on
suke
kuda
OH, PLEASE DON'T DO IT--!!
IF YOU CLOSE IT, I'LL NEVER BE ABLE TO GET HOME!!
SSLUMPP
I'M STUCK INSIDE THE BOOK!!
--MY EXIT'S BEEN SHUT OFF!!
YOU'RE KID-DING!

TA MA HO ME
CHAPTER FOUR
THE SEVEN CONSTELLATIONS OF SUZAKU

TMP TMP
CITY CE
LIBR
MIAKA..
MIAKA...
WHERE IS SHE!?
HUF HUF
BEEP BEEEP

The Universe of the Four Gods
Japanese Translation by Einosuke Okuda
I CAN'T BELIEVE THIS!
I'M TRAPPED INSIDE THIS STORY.
WILL I EVER BE ABLE TO GO HOME? WHAT ABOUT KEISUKE AND MOM?
YUI...
I MISS YOU.

I MAY NEVER SEE TOKYO AGAIN !!
THE BOOKSTORE NEAR THE STATION WHERE WE'D ALWAYS HANG OUT...
KAWAHARA BOOKSTORE
SCHOOL... MY CLASSMATES...
EVEN THAT HORRIBLE CRAM SCHOOL.
I DID IT! I *FORCED* HER OUT OF THE HOUSE !!
HOW THE WORLD WORKS IN MIAKA'S IMAGINATION
NOW OUR UPDATE ON THE MISSING JUNIOR HIGH SCHOOL GIRL. EXAM PRESSURE IS REPORTED TO BE THE CAUSE...
HOW MANY DAYS HAS IT BEEN SINCE I CAME HERE? I BET RIGHT NOW...
MOTHER...

AND... AND...

WHAT-EVER SHALL I DO ABOUT UNDER-WEAR!?

A TRUE TRAGEDY.

YOU MAKE SOME GREAT FACES!

THONK

T--TAMAHOME! HOW DARE YOU SNEAK INTO MY ROOM!!

C'MON! I'M HERE TO CHEER YOU UP! HIS MAJESTY'S WORRIED ABOUT YOU, TOO.

THEY'RE LETTING ME STAY HERE IN THE PALACE, THANKS TO YOU.
...
THE ENTIRE EMPIRE'S GONE GA-GA OVER YOU... MISS PRIESTESS OF SUZAKU!

YOU DON'T HAVE TO KEEP ME COMPANY. IT'S NOT LIKE I'M *LONELY* OR ANYTHING.

HUGGG

EH-HH..

DON'T PRETEND...

WHEN IT'S TIME TO CRY, CRY WITH ALL YOUR HEART.
THAT'S THE FIRST STEP TOWARD FEELING BETTER.
SPECIAL OFFER, FREE OF CHARGE. I'LL BE YOUR BIG BROTHER, ALL RIGHT?
CHSHH
HE'S SO WARM...
BUT HE'S JUST A CHARACTER IN SOME WEIRD BOOK...
Y'KNOW, I WAS THINKING. IF YOU REALLY WANT TO GO HOME...
...ALL YOU GOTTA DO IS GET YOURSELF THE POWER OF THE SUZAKU, RIGHT?
......
YOU COULD BE BACK IN YOUR WORLD IN NO TIME FLAT.

MIAKA!
THAT'S RIGHT!
I'M SORRY. I'VE BEEN SO BUSY...
...I COULDN'T SPEND ANY TIME WITH YOU.
OH NO, NOT AT ALL, HOTO-HORI... I MEAN, YOUR MAJESTY!
SAY, I WAS WONDERING HOW I COULD OBTAIN THE POWERS OF THE SUZAKU.
I WAS RESEARCHING THAT NOW IN *THE UNIVERSE OF THE FOUR GODS.*
U-U-UNIVERSE OF THE FOUR GODS!?
THAT'S THE BOOK WE'RE *IN!*
YES, IT'S A BOOK OF PROPHESIES HANDED DOWN FROM TAI YI-JUN TO HIS MAJESTY TAI JU.*

THE FIRST EMPEROR OF HOTOHORI'S DYNASTY.

IN THE BOOK THERE ARE 28 HOLY CONSTELLATIONS OF HEAVEN <THE 28 CELESTIALS>. EACH OF THE FOUR CARDINAL POINTS, NORTH, SOUTH, EAST AND WEST CLAIMS SEVEN CONSTELLATIONS.
THE SOUTHERN SEVEN CONSTELLATIONS ARE CALLED "THE SUZAKU." IT'S A GENERAL ASTRONOMICAL TERM.
AND I THOUGHT IT WAS SOME KINDA GOD OF BIRDS.
THE NAMES OF THE SEVEN CONSTELLATIONS ARE...
CHICHIRI TAMAHOME
井 鬼
NURIKO HOTOHORI CHIRIKO
柳 星 張
TASUKI MITSUKAKE
翼 軫
THEY MAKE UP THE SOUTHERN SEVEN CONSTELLATIONS, SUZAKU.
TAMAHOME AND HOTOHORI !?
THAT'S CORRECT.

I, HOTOHORI <THE WATER SNAKE>, AND TAMAHOME <CANCER>, AND THE REST OF THE SEVEN CONSTELLATIONS MUST PROTECT...
SHTT
...THE PRIESTESS OF SUZAKU SO THAT SHE CAN OBTAIN HER MAGICAL POWERS.
OH MY
TAMAHOME SUDDENLY APPEARED
YOU MUST FIND THE OTHER FIVE. UNLESS YOU PERSONALLY GATHER ALL SEVEN YOU WILL NOT OBTAIN THE POWERS OF THE SUZAKU.
SAYS SO RIGHT HERE.
WHAT IS THIS? SOME ROLE-PLAYING GAME !?
GET A GRIP
S-SO THEN... THERE ARE FIVE OTHER PEOPLE WHO HAVE SIGNS APPEARING ON THEIR BODIES!?
ACCORDING TO THE BOOK, THE YOUNG LADY WHO GATHERS TOGETHER THE "SEVEN CONSTELLATIONS OF SUZAKU" WILL HAVE HER EVERY WISH GRANTED.
DID YOU KNOW ABOUT THIS, TAMAHOME !?!
I KNEW MY NAME CAME FROM A CONSTELLATION, BUT...
SO I'M SUPPOSED TO PROTECT YOU, HUH??

IN LESS THAN THREE MONTHS I HAVE TO TAKE MY HIGH SCHOOL ENTRANCE EXAMS !!

UH-OH!

IF I DON'T FIND THE OTHER FIVE BY THEN...

HELD BACK

NO WONDER...

...THEY'VE BEEN SO KIND TO ME.

NO WAY! WHERE ART THOU, CONSTELLATION NUMBER THREE ??

HOLD ON. THERE'S A CLUE IN THE BOOK.

AREN'T YOU LISTENING ??

THE THIRD CONSTELLATION IS REFERRED TO BY THE CHARACTERS GONG AND WU. THE FIRST ONE MEANS PALACE AND THE SECOND MEANS FIERCE STRENGTH.

武

SO WHEN WE FIND THE MOST VALIANT MAN IN THE PALACE, WE'LL HAVE FOUND THE THIRD OF OUR SEVEN CONSTELLATIONS.

YOUR MAJESTY, YOUR EMINENCE, AS INSTRUCTED, WE HAVE SELECTED THE FINEST WARRIORS IN THE PALACE.

WELL, I'D RATHER HAVE FIVE BUFF GUYS, SO THERE!
HMPH
EXCUSE MY LACK OF BABE-ITTUDE.
PERSON-ALLY I'D HAVE PREFERRED THE OTHER FIVE TO BE HOT BABES.
VOSHHH
...NOW THEN !!
SHA-KOWW
GRTCH
H-- HE'S GOT STYLE !
THO-WAAKK

KER-
TMP
HUH
??

TAMAHOME... OUR PURPOSE WAS NOT TO ALLOW YOU TO SHOW OFF.

HMM.
LOOKS LIKE IT'S MY TURN.
WH-WHAT THE--

AND WHAT MIGHT YOU HAVE IN MIND?
I'LL BE FINE! THE ONLY THING MY TEACHERS EVER COMPLIMENTED ME ON WAS MY SPEED!

DODGEBALL

SHE'S THE ONLY ONE LEFT.
HUFF HUFF
MIAKA, TRY TO CATCH IT FOR ONCE!

SCHOOL COMPETITIONS

1

DOESN'T THAT JUST PROVE YOU'RE A GLUTTON ??

BESIDES, A TRULY VALIANT MAN WOULD NEVER TOUCH A GIRL.
IN THE SAME WAY BRAVE DOGS DON'T BARK TOO MUCH.
WATCH.
SNK
KANG-LIN, WE HAVE TO GO BACK!
WE'LL BE SCOLDED FOR BEING HERE!
WHY IS SHE SO FRIENDLY WITH HIS MAJESTY? SHE'S NO EMPRESS!
AND WHO IS THE MAN NEXT TO THEM?
HE IS ONE OF THE PROTECTORS OF THE PRIESTESS. A CELESTIAL WARRIOR OF SUZAKU, TAMAHOME.
SO THAT'S THE PRIESTESS OF SUZAKU EVERYONE'S BEEN TALKING ABOUT?

DON'T JUST STAND THERE! COME 'N' GET ME.
......
YOUR EMINENCE, WE WOULDN'T DARE HARM YOU.
...
GIVE ME A BREAK.
HIDING BEHIND YOUR BEARDS AND YOUR ARMOR!
ADMIT IT! YOU'RE ALL ACTUALLY PEEING YOUR PANTS BECAUSE I'M FROM ANOTHER WORLD!
LOSER
LOSER
LOSER
LOSER
LOSER
LOSER
IDIOTS! MORONS! WEAK-LINGS!!
RATTL
RATTL
FRAIDY-CAT! FRAIDY-CAT!
AND YOU CALL YOUR-SELVES WARRIORS!!
BET'CHA CAN'T CATCH ME!!
IS SHE 6 YEARS OLD OR WHAT?

WHY, YOU LITTLE...

TRMBL

TRMBL

NO WARRIOR WOULD PUT UP WITH SUCH INSULTS!!

DAAAAN

BAAAAAAA-

WHOOPS

VONNNGG

ZHOOM

KA-CHOKK

TMP TMP TMP

KRAK RAK RAK RAK

CA-CHONK
CA-CHONK
CHONK
KRAK-RAK
MIAKA! GET AWAY FROM THERE!
YOU JERKS! NEVER TRY TO HURT A GIRL!
POWW
IT'S FALLING APART!!

SKKRK
SKKRK
SHKA-
BASH!
MIAKA!!
CHA-CHING
THAT'LL BE 390 YEN, PLEASE.

YUI, WHAT'D YOU BUY?

A *TEXT-BOOK!!* JUST KIDDING. SOME MANGA.

OH RIGHT.

GENIUSES DON'T HAVE TO STUDY.

MY GOD!!

YUI, WHAT HAP-PENED!?!

HUH??

THERE'S BLOOD ON YOUR SKIRT...

VSHH

WHAT..

UNGG..

OWW
I THINK I INJURED MY LEG...
LOOKS LIKE I'M STILL ALIVE THOUGH.
HURRY! REMOVE THIS RUBBLE NOW!!
MRMR
YOUR MAJESTY, YOU MUSTN'T!
MRMR
LEAVE ME ALONE!!

TAMA... HOME...?
ALL THE WARRIORS ARE UNCONSCIOUS.
WE DON'T HAVE ENOUGH PEOPLE TO MOVE IT--
SO THAT WAS YOU...
FOR A MOMENT I FELT SOMETHING COVERING ME...
KRRRRCH
TAMAHOME! YOU'LL BE CRUSHED! STOP IT!

SO NO MATTER WHAT HAPPENS...
STUPID! I TOLD YOU I'D LOOK AFTER YOU, RIGHT ??
...I'LL ALWAYS PROTECT YOU.
BA-DUMP
CHKLL CHKLL
CHKLL CHKLL

MIAKA! TAMAHOME!
SOMETHING MUST BE DONE!
ALLOW ME TO HANDLE THIS.
TAMAHOME!!
KRTCH
URRGHHH..
DAMN. I CAN'T--
VSHH

KA-THONGG
POT
WAAAHH!
KOMMM
WHAAAM
VWING
HUH ?!
KA-JOKK
WOAH !! WATCH OUT !!
VWIPP
VWIPP
VWIPP
HM HM

Let me just say that drawing the buildings in this chapter was no easy task. I did all this research to draw them (although I didn't want it to look exactly the same as in my reference, so I'd alter some of the designs and layouts). It was a real pain for my assistants but also for me as well. (I do as much of the backgrounds as I possibly can.) Hey, Chinese architecture, why're you such a pain!? And these outfits are no easier. Not to mention the mob scenes. And I've had it up to here with the soldiers' armor! (I was gonna use Romance of the Three Kingdoms as reference material, but that story's set too far back in time. There's not a whole lot of changes over time in China but we're talking about a difference of a thousand years. At least I want the armor to be right. The armor is kind of a pastiche between different periods, mostly the period between the Sung and Ming dynasties but also a little bit of Tang all mixed up together. But this China is supposed to be a work of the imagination. Even my editor's been telling me not to be too particular.

When I was in elementary school I loved the TV live drama show "Saiyuki." Then they started doing reruns when I was eighteen. All of a sudden I realized how great the action, characters, and comedy were. So I'd look forward to 8 p.m. every Sunday. That's really the kind of project I'd like to work on.

By the way, I really wanted to have Tamahome wear an outfit with Chinese buttons, but the style only came into existence in modern China. I might eventually draw it in anyway.

In the first graphic novel, maybe! The kimono style just isn't much fun. When were the "Mr. Vampire" and "Chinese Ghost Story" series set? I'd like Tamahome to wear the same clothes worn by the guy in "Mr. Vampire," but maybe that outfit would be too recent. I know, I know. I'm not supposed to be so particular, but I am. Oh, I also pay a lot of attention to hair. The bun style is just too boring.

ARE YOU TWO ALL RIGHT !?
DOC, I'M DYIN' !!
YOU PROTECTED THE PRINCESS WELL, TAMAHOME!
HE DIDN'T DO "WELL" AT ALL! WHAT WOULD WE DO IF HE DIED-- !?
OH?
I'M ONLY DOING WHAT I FEEL LIKE DOING.
AND EVENTUALLY I'M GOING TO EXPECT SOME EXPENSIVE THANK-YOU GIFTS.
TH-THANKS.

YOUR EMI-NENCE.
YOUR EMINENCE, ARE YOU ALL RIGHT??
I THOUGHT MY HEART WOULD STOP, RIGHT THEN.
TAMA-HOME...
OUCH! TAKE IT EASY, WILL YA?
IS HE PROTECTING ME JUST BECAUSE I'M THE PRIESTESS OF SUZAKU?
THE POWER YOU DIS-PLAYED A MOMENT AGO, COULD THAT POSSIBLY BE...
OR...
ARE YOU AN EMPIRIAL CONSORT FROM THE INNER SERAGLIO?
HE DOESN'T KNOW BECAUSE HE'S NEVER BEEN THERE.

I AM KANG-LIN.
OR "NURIKO" AS IN THE CONSTEL-LATION.
GRIN ♥
POINGG
SO SHE'S A WOMAN !!
GREAT! WE'VE ALREADY FOUND THE THIRD CONSTEL-LATION...
THANK YOU FOR RESCUING ME !
I'M MIAKA YŪKI !! ♥
♥ LET'S SHAKE

THE ONLY ONE I WANTED TO RESCUE WAS HIM!!
TMPTMPTMP
WOOOSH
HMPH
SMA-AKK
T-T-TAMAHOME!!

CHAPTER
FIVE
DANGEROUS LOVE

RESTROOMS
BA-KAAM
YUI, THAT BLOOD-STAIN...
...IS IT...
YOUR TIME OF THE--?
NO! AND I'M NOT INJURED EITHER!
HOW'D IT GET THERE?
SOME-THING'S NOT RIGHT!
IT'S GROSSING ME *OUT!* GO WASH IT OFF!

FSSSSHHAAA
GUCHA GUCHA
IT WON'T COME OFF!
YOU'RE KIDDING! ARE YOU USING SOAP!?
LET ME SEE THAT!
HUH?! YOU'RE RIGHT!
ZHEET
I FINALLY GOT IT OUT!
...
IT... JUST... VAN-ISHED.

OWW!
JTTTT
THAT GIRL, NURIKO...!!
BLOOD-STAINS ARE SO HARD TO WASH OUT!
ESPECIALLY WITHOUT ANY SOAP.
TA-DAHH
WHY DID SHE GO AND KISS TAMAHOME LIKE THAT!?!
GRR GRR
TMP TMP TMP TMP
I'LL START RIGHT AFTER I'M FINISHED DOING LAUNDRY.
SO I'M GONNA HAVE TO MAKE FRIENDS WITH ALL SEVEN OF THEM.
CALM DOWN, MIAKA. THE ONLY WAY TO GET BACK TO MY OWN WORLD IS TO OBTAIN THE POWER OF SUZAKU. TO DO THAT, I GOTTA GATHER ALL SEVEN WARRIORS.

CHA BAMM
MIAKA!
WHUMP
TWIP
FWOH WOH WOH
AIII EEEE!
YOU PLANNED THAT, YOU PER-VERT!
NO NO NO NO NO
I AM NOT! I JUST NEED SOME-PLACE TO HIDE!!
HA HA HA HA HA
IF IT ISN'T MIAKA. SO SORRY TO INTRUDE.

HAHAHA
THIS MAN IS SO SHY.
COME, TAMA-BABY, WE'RE LEAVING. ♥
ZHGHL ZHGHL ZHGHL
ZHGHL ZHGHL
JSH H-TAK
...
HA HA HA HA HA
WHAT IS UP WITH THAT WOMAN !?!
YOU WANT TO BE MY ATTENDANT?
Y-YES MA'AM.
HMM
GET OFF OF ME!
STRGL
STRGL STRGL

KRAAK KRAAK
GWUMPH
...YOU MUST NEVER INTERFERE IN OUR RELATIONSHIP.
BUT...
YOU CAN IF YOU WANT.
PHEW
MIAKA... COME HELP ME WITH MY HAIR.
OH, TAMAHOME! YOU SAID YOU WOULD ALWAYS PROTECT ME.
YOU'RE PUTTY IN HER HANDS!
NEVER EVEN ENTERED MY MIND!
CHOKE
GRR GRR

YOU'RE HURTING ME! DON'T PULL SO HARD!
SPLATCH

FWUSH

PLTTA PLTTA PLTTA
RUBB RUBB RUBB

CLEAN IT UP.
IF YOU MISS ANY SPOTS, YOU'LL GET NO DINNER.
IT'S DUSTY OUT HERE.

I'M SORRY! I LOST MY GRIP...
KER-THUNK
THAT'S NOT FAIR--!!

WHAT!?!
THAT'S THE DIRTIEST FLOOR I'VE EVER SEEN!
NO DINNER FOR YOU!

ME !??
BOO HOO
HEY, QUIT PICKIN' ON MIAKA.
Y'KNOW, I JUST DON'T LIKE--

V-V-VERY DISTURBING BEHAVIOR--
TAMA-BABY, FORGET THE USELESS WENCH. LET'S GO HAVE DINNER. ♥
GRKL GRKL

GWUMPH
I'M SO HAPPY!
KRAKL KRAKL

NOW, WAIT! I NEVER SAID I DIDN'T LIKE YOU!
YOU DON'T LIKE ME!!
I'M NOT GOOD ENOUGH! YOU WANT THE LITTLE FLAKE! YOU WANT THE LITTLE TWIT!

THEN... THEN YOU LIKE ME!?

GRR——RRRR

GRR GRR GRR GR GRR GR

GROWL
GRR OWL
I AM SO HUNGRY!
THAT NURIKO IS SUCH A PAIN IN THE BUTT.
FWAKAMM
TAMA-HOME, YOU JERK!!
SHE MUST REALLY LIKE TAMA-HOME, THOUGH.
TAMA--
STRGL
STRGL
HUFF HUFF!
...
STRGL STRGL STRGL STRGL

HEY, I THOUGHT YOU'D FAINTED-- !?
HUFF HUFF
I LAID LOW UNTIL SHE LEFT THE ROOM. THEN I CRAWLED OUT.
YOU MUST BE PSYCHED WITH A *BABE* LIKE THAT DROOLING AFTER YOU.
DON'T BE A MORON! YOU THINK I'M *HAPPY* ABOUT THIS !?
I'M JUST BEING NICE 'CAUSE SHE'S A WOMAN AND ONE OF THE WARRIORS.
I'M NOT LISTENING!

So I was reading some fan mail informing me that Prepubescence was voted second place in the top 20 manga poll of an anime magazine in Taiwan (I think). *Can it really be true?* A friend in the bookstore business told me that it was ranked in the top 10, 20, 30, or something. I dunno what it was, but I'm just happy to be ranked! SNIFFL SNIFFL Thank you everyone, so much!
I received some fan mail from Taiwan, from a 15-year-old named Li. So I have readers abroad! A girl who was half Chinese and half Japanese wrote me when I was working on "Treasure of the Heart," Yui Len (I could have the wrong spelling), and she's studying martial arts with a real master. That's awesome! Her name is so cute, I'll have to use it in a future manga.
I once got a letter from someone who's half British/half Japanese... Very international. I have to admit I'm a little nervous about having native Chinese reading Fushigi Yûgi.
Oh, and thanks so much for the tapes. *I'm changing the subject.* I listen to them all! There's B'z, TMN, Ranma soundtracks, recorded letters, Lodoss soundtracks, etc. Oh, when I mentioned COCO in Prepubescence I had lots of people writing back! They're really popular! A special thanks to the people who made compilation tapes of COCO songs dedicated to scenes in Prepubescence. They were great! It's true that "Your Song, My Song" is really appropriate as Manato's song right around the "to live in the present" scene. "Melody" is perfect for that scene where Asuka is hiding in the rain, watching Manato. The best song though is "Circus Game"!! I was thinking how much I wanted it to be the theme song! But I found out that the "No Interest in Prepubescence" CD is coming out!! I'm on it too, so please listen to it. For those who are just now being introduced to my work, "No Interest in Prepubescence" is a three volume comic. Check it out!! ♥

But why wasn't the COCO tune "Why?" on the tape. "Why?" Oh, I get it, just so I'd make a silly pun.

WOAH!
VVOMP
THE WOUND ON MY LEG!
HUH? WHY'D YOU FALL DOWN!?!
KA-LUMP
IT'S NOTHING!
DON'T MOVE.
YOU'RE BLEEDING AGAIN.
I BROUGHT SOME OINTMENT AND BANDAGES JUST IN CASE.
I ALWAYS COME PREPARED.
BA-DUMP
O-OKAY.

NURIKO WOULD BE FURIOUS IF SHE SAW US LIKE THIS.
I FEEL KINDA GUILTY.

SO DO YOU LIKE NURIKO?
NO WAY! I ONLY MET HER YESTERDAY.
BESIDES, SHE'S NOT MY TYPE.

REALLY? YOU HAVE NO FEELINGS WHATSO-EVER?
...

I SEE!
I GET IT.
HEH HEH

YOU'RE JEALOUS!
I REALIZE THAT I'M A KIND, MACHO, BEEFCAKE OF A MARTIAL ARTIST...
HAHAHAHA
CAREFUL, GIRL, I'M A HEART-BREAKER!!
...BUT MONEY IS MY FIRST LOVE.
I... I'M NOT JEALOUS!!

MIAKA, COULD YOU COME OVER HERE?

WHAT IS IT? ALL OF THE SUDDEN.

SOME TIME AGO, I LOST A VERY PRECIOUS EARRING WHILE I WAS TAKING A WALK NEAR THE POND.

OH!
YOU WANT *ME* TO GO GET IT?

OH, *WOULD* YOU !?
IN RETURN I PROMISE TO SERVE AS ONE OF THE SEVEN CELESTIAL WARRIORS OF SUZAKU.
SURE!
I'LL BE BACK IN A SEC.

HMF!
FOOL!

WHAT WAS THAT?
I WASN'T LISTENING.
AS I WAS SAYING...
YOUR MAJESTY IS EIGHTEEN. IT IS TIME TO CONSIDER MARRIAGE.
OUR PUBLIC OFFICIALS HAVE GONE TO GREAT TROUBLE TO GATHER BEAUTIFUL WOMEN FROM ALL OVER THE EMPIRE. WHY DO YOU IGNORE THE WOMEN OF THE INNER SERAGLIO?
HMPH!
WE ARE FAR MORE BEAUTIFUL THAN THEY.
THAT WAS A JOKE.
EVEN THO IT'S TRUE.
SHOULD WE NOT BE CONCENTRATING ON THE STATE OF THE EMPIRE?
BUT...
THAT'S RIGHT! HOW ABOUT THAT GIRL, NURIKO?
NONSENSE. SHE IS ONE OF THE SEVEN CELESTIAL WARRIORS, AND AS SUCH HAS BEEN RELEASED FROM THE SERAGLIO TO SERVE MIAKA.

BOO!
SINCE CHILD-HOOD, WE'VE HAD AN IMAGE.
WE KNOW THE FACE OF OUR IDEAL WOMAN.
AND SHE IS...
MIAKA, WHAT ARE YOU DOING HERE?
I KNEW I COULDN'T SCARE YOU!
I WAS JUST ON MY WAY TO DO A FAVOR FOR NURIKO.
JUST PASSING THRU.
AREN'T YOU TWO GETTING ALONG? I CAN ORDER HER TO--
NO, WE'RE FINE. BE-SIDES...

I WANT TO MAKE FRIENDS WITH HER ON MY OWN.
I'M ON MY WAY.
FSH HA
MIAKA...!
K-TMP
K-TMP
...YOU CAN'T ORDER SOMEONE'S FEELINGS TO CHANGE!
!!

FSHAAAA
AII IIEE!!
I CAN'T SEE A THING HERE...
SHVR
K-TMP
SWISHHHH
LOOSH
ZHAA
YAAAAAHH!
KA-CHAK
I'M HOME.

TA-CHUNK

OF COURSE, I'M THE ONLY ONE HOME.
COMES WITH THE TURF WITH A LATCH-KEY KID.

WHAT A WEIRD DAY THOUGH-- WHAT WAS THAT BLOOD?

BLOOSH

....

PL-DIPP

PL-DIPP

DID MIAKA WIND UP OVER THERE !?!
SHE RAN OUT AND HASN'T BEEN HOME SINCE!
GLUP BLUP
GLORPH
GLORPH
THE SEAWEED'S GOT ME...
GLORPH
I CAN'T BREATHE!!
JHEET
GABLOPH
TAMA... HOME...!

ZZZZ
POIT
MIAKA...!...?
DAMN. WHEN DID I DRIFT OFF?
IT'S COLD TONIGHT.
WHAT HAP-PENED TO MIAKA??
I COULDA *SWORN* I HEARD HER CALLING ME.
TMP TMP TMP
HAHAHAHAHA
WHAT A *FOOL* THAT GIRL IS!
TWRL
HAHAHAHA
SHE WENT TO GO SEARCH FOR A *NON-EXISTENT* EARRING IN THAT COLD, COLD POND.
I WAS RESTRICTED TO THE INNER BUILDINGS. HOW COULD I HAVE EVER GONE NEAR THE POND IN THE *FIRST* PLACE?
SHE'S PROBABLY FREEZING IN THE COLD WATER RIGHT NOW!

KURCH
WHAM
THAT'LL TEACH HER--
ZHI-GNIKKK
...GONNA DROWN !!
I AM NOT...
DAMMIT !!
DID YOU SAY WHAT I THOUGHT YOU SAID-- !?

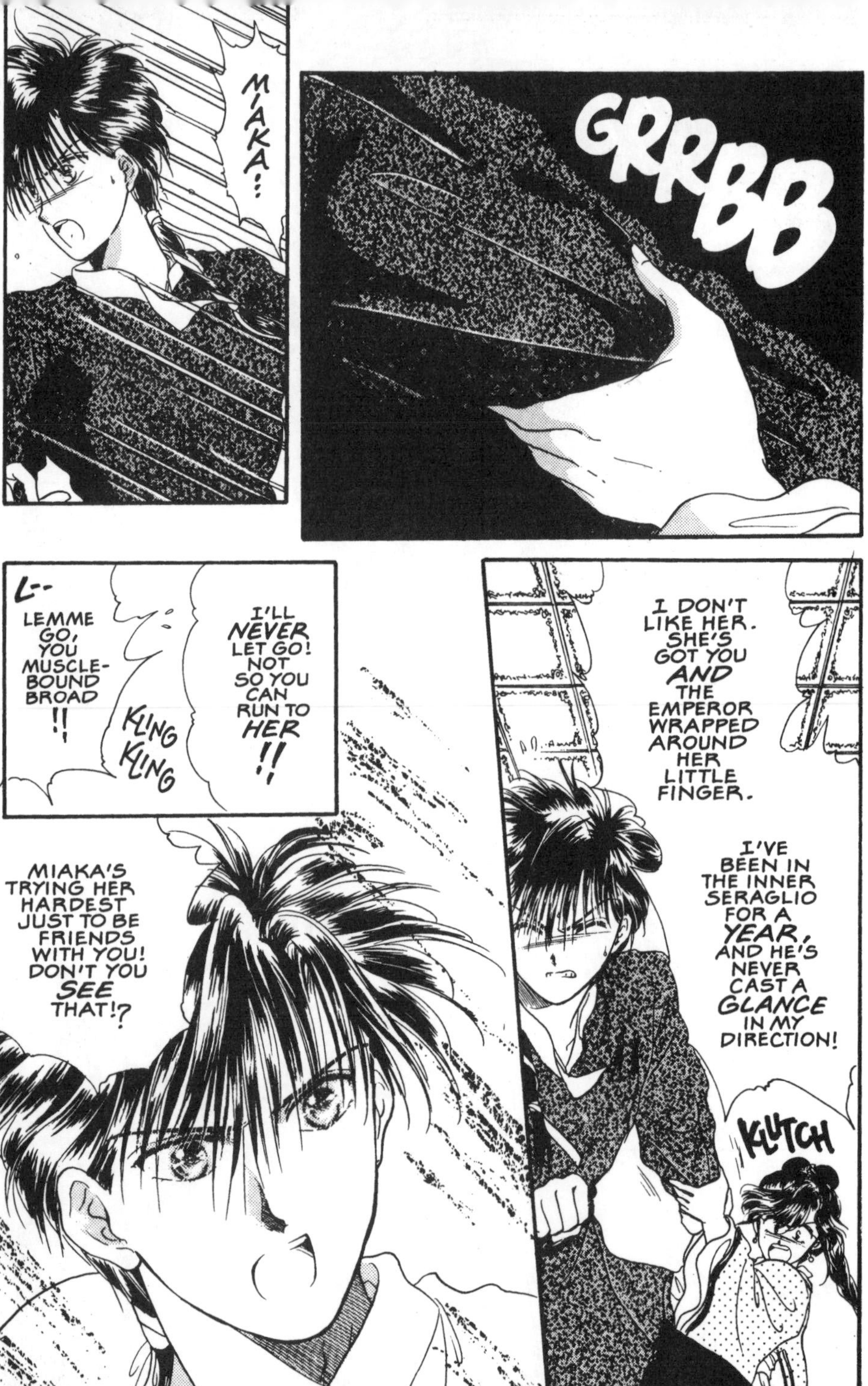

I DON'T LIKE HER. SHE'S GOT YOU *AND* THE EMPEROR WRAPPED AROUND HER LITTLE FINGER.

I'VE BEEN IN THE INNER SERAGLIO FOR A *YEAR*, AND HE'S NEVER CAST A *GLANCE* IN MY DIRECTION!

KLUTCH

I'LL *NEVER* LET GO! NOT SO YOU CAN RUN TO *HER*!!

LEMME GO, YOU MUSCLE-BOUND BROAD!!

KLING KLING

MIAKA'S TRYING HER HARDEST JUST TO BE FRIENDS WITH YOU! DON'T YOU *SEE* THAT!?

YOU'RE IN LOVE WITH HOTOHORI... WITH HIS MAJESTY?
SO I DECIDED TO GET REVENGE BY STEALING YOU!!
AND HIS MAJESTY JUST DOTES ON HER!? WHAT'S SO GOOD ABOUT A LITTLE TWERP FROM ANOTHER WORLD!?
THEN SHE COMES OUT OF NOWHERE AND GETS THE ROYAL TREATMENT!
THAT EXPLAINS IT...
PL-DIPP PL-DIPP
RLIPP RLIPP
IT CAN'T BE...
MIAKA! YOU'RE ALL RIGHT!?
ISN'T IT PRETTY?
HERE.
THERE WAS NO EARRING THERE, SO INSTEAD I FOUND THIS STONE.

YOUR STORY DIDN'T ADD UP. YOU SAID YOURSELF YOU WEREN'T ALLOWED OUTSIDE THE BUILDING.

YOU LITTLE *FOOL!* YOU WENT INTO THE POND!? I WAS LYING.

I KNEW THAT...

THWHAP

I WON'T BE MOCKED!!

DON'T WORRY, THERE'S NOTHING GOING ON BETWEEN HOTOHORI AND ME!

SO YOU WERE *JEALOUS* OF ME !!

TWRLL

SO WHAT'M I? CHOPPED LIVER?!

AND ??

YOU WANT ME TO HELP OUT? I CAN TALK TO HOTOHORI FOR YOU.

SHE *DOESN'T* HAVE A CRUSH ON TAMAHOME !!

YOU'RE PROBABLY SUR-ROUNDED BY WOMEN IN LOVE WITH YOU.
"AND..." IT'D BE NICE IF YOU WERE MORE CON-SIDERATE TOWARDS THEM.
HER CLOTHES ARE WET, THUS... THE ROBE.
AND WHAT ABOUT YOU? IS THERE A MAN YOU'RE IN LOVE WITH?
BA-DUMP
M-ME--?
SHOOM
DON'T WORRY ABOUT ME. I JUST WANTED TO RECOM-MEND SOMEONE IN PARTICULAR FOR YOU.

FUKUSHHHH
HUH?
SOMEONE I'VE CHERISHED SINCE TIME BEGAN.
SINCE BEFORE I CAN REMEMBER...
I ALREADY HAVE SOME-ONE.

CHAPTER SIX
HIDDEN LOVE

I ALWAYS WONDERED WHAT SHE WOULD BE LIKE.
EVER SINCE I WAS A CHILD, I'VE HEARD STORIES OF THE PRIESTESS OF SUZAKU WHO COMES TO US FROM ANOTHER WORLD.
BA-DUMP
BA-DUMP
BA-DUMP
BA-DUMP
BA-DUMP
H-- HOLD ON A SEC.
I'M STILL IN JUNIOR HIGH.
MIAKA...
YOU'RE EXACTLY HOW I IMAGINED YOU'D BE. NO OTHER WOMAN HOLDS ANY INTEREST FOR ME.
BA-DUMP
BA-DUMP

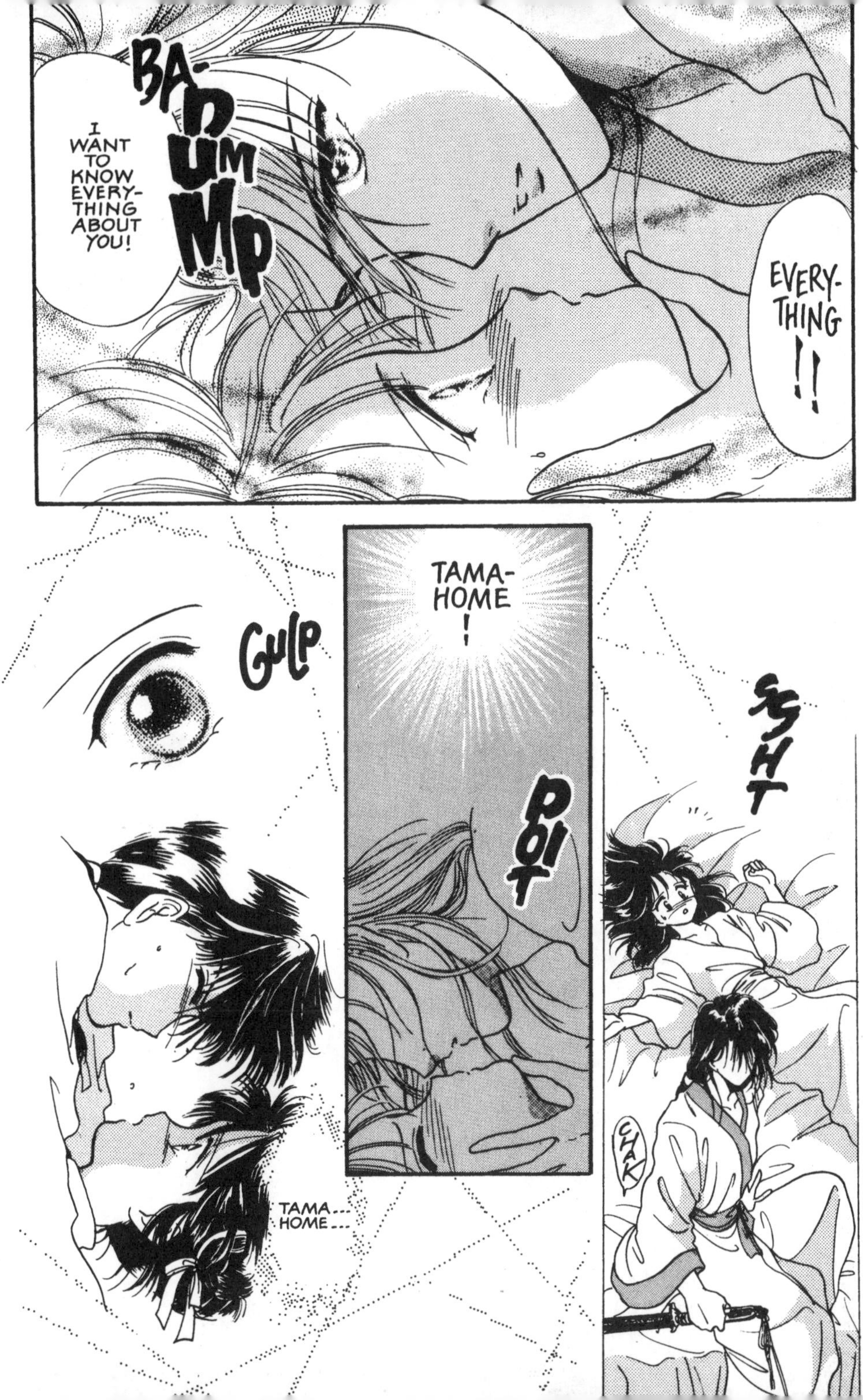

EVERY-THING!!
I WANT TO KNOW EVERY-THING ABOUT YOU!
BA-DUMUMP
TAMA-HOME!
GULP
POIT
SSHT
CHAK
TAMA... HOME...

CHSSHHT
WHAT? WHAT IS HE DOING !?!
TMP TMP TMP TMP
ZWISHHT
ZWISHHT
ZWWISHHT
KA-CHKK
KA-CHKK
T-- TAMAHOME! NURIKO !!

LA LA LA LA LA LA
WHAT BRINGS YOU TWO HERE?
YOU CAN STOP DANCING NOW.

WE HAVE COME FOR MIAKA, YOUR MAJESTY.

AS YOU WISH...

WHILE IT IS TRUE, I *HAVE* GRANTED YOU ACCESS TO MY PRIVATE APARTMENTS...

...PERHAPS YOU *COULD* USE MORE DISCRETION.

HMPH

PANG

MIAKA.
TMP TMP TMP
H-H-HOTOHORI! I SHOULD BE RETURNING TO MY ROOM, TOO...
YOU SAID YOU WANT TO RETURN TO YOUR WORLD, BUT...
I MEANT WHAT I SAID.
...AS SOON AS SUZAKU ARRIVES AND THIS ENTIRE ORDEAL IS OVER, I WILL MAKE YOU MY EMPRESS.

HEY, YOU CAN'T PUSH ME ARO--
OF COURSE, IT WILL NOT BE BY DECREE.
I'LL MAKE SURE YOU FALL IN LOVE WITH ME.
I-- I CAN'T BE-LIEVE THIS !!
WHO COULD STOP HIM?
DI-NG-DO-NG
CHRP CHRP
HE JUST PRO-POSED TO ME !!
NOT A WINK OF SLEEP.

DEEPLY TROUBLED
TAMA-HOME HEARD ALL THAT. I WONDER WHAT HE'S THINK-ING...
WHAT AM I GONNA DO? DOESN'T HE REALIZE I HAVE TO GET OUT OF THIS BOOK AND TAKE MY ENTRANCE EXAMS?!
DOES THIS ALL HAPPEN IN THE BOOK? DOES SOME GORGEOUS GUY PROPOSE TO THE HEROINE?
YO...
UM
UM
WHADDLE I DO?
POING
SHHFFT

"YO"? THAT'S IT!?
AREN'T YOU GONNA SAY SOMETHING ABOUT LAST NIGHT?
WH-- WHERE ARE YOU GOING??
GOTTA GO DOWNTOWN AND MAKE SOME MONEY.
I CAME FROM THE PROVINCES FOR WORK BUT I HAVEN'T HAD A SECOND FOR MYSELF.
TMP TMP TMP
WAIT! I'LL GO TOO!
WHY DON'T YOU TEAM UP WITH NURIKO AND GO FIND THE OTHER FOUR CONSTELLATIONS?
GAK!
NURIKO...
MI-A-KA...!!
BWAAAH
AIIEEEEEEE!
LOOK AT HER BATTLE AURA SPARK!

I WILL NEVER FORGIVE YOU !!
IS THIS WHAT YOU MEAN BY "THERE'S NOTHING GOING ON BETWEEN HOTOHORI AND ME" ?
BWWAAHH

IF HE'S GONNA BE THAT WAY...
A-AND I THOUGHT WE WERE ON THE VERGE OF BEING FRIENDS...
TAMA-BABY, HOLD ON! I'M COMING WITH YOU!

HOW MUCH FOR--
I'LL TAKE THIS--
HE COULD HAVE SAID SOME-THING! DOESN'T HE CARE ABOUT ME !?
AND HOW COULD TAMAHOME GIVE ME THE COLD SHOULDER LIKE THAT !?
GRR
GRR GRR

SNEEK SNEEK
...I REALLY WANNA BE FRIENDS WITH NURIKO. AND I NEED TO KNOW HOW TAMAHOME FEELS!
I HATE FOLLOWING PEOPLE AROUND, BUT...
...
GRR GRR GRR
I CAN'T BELIEVE NURIKO. I KNOW SHE'S IN LOVE WITH HOTOHORI, BUT SHE'S HANGING ALL OVER TAMAHOME!
TMP
LADIES AND GENTLEMEN!!
TAMA-BABY, LOOK AT THAT GIRL'S CHILDISH DISGUISE!
LEAVE HER BE.
YOU'RE SO STERN!

WHAT'S GOING ON?
WHO'S HE--?
WHAT'S HE SELLING?
YOU'VE ALL HEARD ABOUT THE PRIESTESS OF SUZAKU, RIGHT??
AND YOU KNOW THAT THE PRIESTESS COMES FROM AN ENTIRELY DIFFERENT WORLD.
YEAH? WHAT ABOUT IT!?
EVERYTHING, HER CLOTHES, HER POSSESSIONS... ARE FROM THIS OTHER WORLD!
LADIES AND GENTLEMEN, HAVE I GOT A TREAT FOR YOU! A LIMITED TIME OFFER OF ONE OF HER PRIZE POSSESSIONS!
HE CAN'T MEAN--
PRESENTING:
TA-DAH!!
GUM
WOAAAH!
IT'S GOT SOME FOREIGN WRITING ON IT!!
THAT'S THE CHEWING GUM I GAVE HIM!
SO HE STILL HAD IT ON HIM.

TAMA-HOME
WE'LL START THE BIDDING AT ONE SILVER RYO PER STICK!
THAT'S TOO MUCH!

MAYBE ALL HE SEES ME AS IS AN OPPORTUNITY TO MAKE SOME MONEY.

WHY WOULD YOU HAVE ANYTHING OF HER EMINENCE'S ??
THERE'S SOMETHING FISHY GOIN' ON HERE.

THAT'S RIGHT! THAT'S RIGHT !!
SOMEBODY COULDA SCRIBBLED WRITING ON THERE AND TRIED TO PASS IT OFF AS THE REAL THING!
WE JUST DON'T KNOW IF IT'S REAL!

HEY, YOU TRYING TO SMEAR MY TAMA-BABY!?
GATCH
URGH

I HEARD THE PRIESTESS LIVES IN THE EMPEROR'S PALACE !
HMM

TAMA-HOME IS NOT THAT KIND OF MAN!!
I GAVE HIM THAT GUM, PERSONALLY!!
WHOOOSSHH
UH-OH
MIAKA.
IT'S THE PRIESTESS...
OH MY GOD...
THE PRIESTESS OF SUZAKU?
OH, NO!!

AAAAHHHH

IT'S THE *REAL* PRIESTESS OF SUZAKU!!

OH M'GOD OH M'GOD

LIKE, PEACE, DUDES

ALL RIGHT, ALL RIGHT. EVERYBODY GET IN LINE. EVERYONE WILL GET A CHANCE FOR AN AUTOGRAPH. AN AUTOGRAPH *AND* A HANDSHAKE WILL BE ONE GOLD RYO!

WHEN DID *YOU* BECOME MY MANAGER!?

SAY, COME TO THINK OF IT, I SAW HIM WITH THE PRIESTESS LAST TIME!

ME TOO! GIMME ONE!

THEN SHE MUST BE THE *REAL* THING!

GWUMPH

GIMME ONE OF THAT GUB STUFF!!

TSK

SNEEK SNEEK SNEEK

HU FF
HU FF
HU FF
QUASHH
QUISH
W-WAIT FOR ME...
HU FF
HU FF
!
FWISH
YOU IDIOT... WHAT DID YOU THINK YOU WERE DOING?
YOU BLEW YOUR COVER.
B-BUT-- BUT--

THEN HOW DO YOU FEEL ABOUT ME !?
AM I JUST IN YOUR WAY ?
I NEVER SAID ANYTHING LIKE THAT !
...BUT WE GOT BUSINESS TO DISCUSS WITH YOU.
SORRY TO INTER-RUPT THE LOVE SCENE...

HUFF
HUFF
JEEZ, MIAKA!!
HUFF
HUFF
WHERE'D YOU GO OFF TO?
YUI!
KEISUKE! I JUST GOT OFF THE PHONE WITH YOUR MOTHER! DID MIAKA REALLY RUN AWAY!?
THEY WERE FIGHTING OVER HER ENTRANCE EXAMS!
MIAKA'S BEEN WORKING SO HARD! MOM CAN JUST BE A *DEMON* WHEN IT COMES TO GRADES!

BA-DUMP

TMP

!?

MAYBE MIAKA WENT BACK TO THE LIBRARY!

The Universe of the Four Gods
Japanese Translation by Einosuke Okuda

WHAT "BUSINESS"?

YOU WANNA WORK IN THIS TOWN, YOU GOTTA PAY FOR YOUR PROTECTION!

YOU JERKS! YOU THINK I GOT THAT KIND OF MONEY??

PLUS I LOST ALL MY GUM TO THAT CROWD.

SO THEY'RE JUST LOCAL MOB.
I GUESS YOU CAN FIND THEM ANYWHERE.
GRABB
GAAKK!!
CUTE BROAD.
TWRL
BOSS!
!
IS HE HUMAN??
LET GO OF HER!!
WHAAHH!
"PRINGLE-HEAD, ONCE YOU POP YOU JUST CAN'T STOP."TM

Fushigi Yûgi ∾ 1

Oops, my handwriting's getting sloppy again. Now here's something that caught me by surprise! I never thought you guys would like Tamahome with long hair!! When Tamahome's hair was trimmed shorter in this episode, the complaints came rushing in! I thought you'd prefer short hair, but boy was I wrong!! Tama's action scenes are hard to draw with his long hair. Don't worry, I'll never cut Hotohori's hair (my assistants and I call him "Ho-ri"). Apparently, the fans are divided between the Tamahome faction and Hotohori faction.

I would never have believed your average junior high (and elementary) school student would be into Hotohori. Surprise! Which one will Miaka choose? I really can't portray a girl who can't decide on the guy she's in love with. I like a girl who's got her mind set on one guy. ♥♥ To say you like both guys equally only means that you aren't really in love with either of them. *Although she herself might not even be aware of it.* Well, let's not be too judgmental here.

I know I've said that I don't want any official fan club, but there are still people who want to join! Hmm, some people insisted on forming their own club and asked me how to let the entire country know about it. I got an idea! I'll print your address right here so everybody can see it! What do you think?? TA-DAHH Just kidding. You'd be so flooded with applications that you'd have a heart attack! (I'm not really that popular, though.) Anyway, for your sake I won't mention it.

Now, I heard there're people making their own Fushigi Yûgi dojinshi manga. That's okay, but be sure you send them to me too, okay? I'll be waiting to see them. ♥

Until we meet again.

LISTEN, YOU TWO! YOUR PROTECTION RACKET IS GETTING OUTTA HAND. TAKE THIS AND SCRAM!
YOU ARE A MAN OF BUSINESS, RIGHT? YOU CAME HERE TO MAKE MONEY, RIGHT?
I'M IN THE BUSINESS OF TRADE FOR PROFIT, TOO.

SNEEKS

THIS IS TROUBLE FOR MIAKA AND TAMA-BABY!

I'M SUCH A NICE PERSON, I'LL ACT AS A WITNESS! ♥

SHE'S BEING A MEANIE.

I'LL GIVE YOU A FULL THIRTY GOLD RYO FOR HER!

SELL ME THE GIRL!

Y-- YOU DARE TO INSULT ME!!

GET A REAL FACE, MR. POTATO-CHIP HEAD!

T-T-TAMA-HOME !!
THAT'S WAY TOO CHEAP!
I CAN'T BELIEVE THIS...
FORTY !!
NOT EVEN CLOSE.
KEEP IT COMIN'! YOU'RE GETTIN' WARMER!
HOW ABOUT THIRTY-FIVE !!
I HATE YOU...
I'M NOT GONNA TAKE MUCH MORE OF THIS!
TRY ME ONCE MORE !!
HOW COULD YOU !??

TAMAHOME!!
OUCHIE !!

SNIKT
ZZAT
TAMA-HOME !!
BAS-TARD !!
THO-ONK
KRAAKK
FA-CHA

YOU IDIOTS. NO MATTER HOW MUCH YOU'RE WILLING TO PAY...
KA-WHUMP
TMP
...SOME THINGS ARE PRICE-LESS!
NOW YOU CAN'T DO BUSINESS IN THIS TOWN!
WHY ARE YOU DOING THIS FOR ME!?
LET'S GO, MIAKA.
THAT WAS A STUPID THING TO DO!

TELL ME !
CAN'T YOU SEE THAT I'M FALLING IN LOVE WITH YOU!?
IT DOESN'T MATTER.
IT DOES TO ME !
OH, M'GOD !!

.....
SORRY...
...BUT I CAN'T SAY THAT I FEEL THE SAME.
I'M JUST PROTECTING YOU BECAUSE YOU'RE THE PRIESTESS OF SUZAKU.

TO BE CONTINUED IN VOLUME 2: ORACLE